WO 634/258

MOST
SECRET

GHQ AUXILIARY
UNITS

SEPT 1943 — JULY 1944

TO BE KEPT UNDER LOCK AND KEY

It is requested that special care may be taken
to ensure the secrecy of this document.

BEWLEY DOWN

2011

SELAH
Plate 1

BEWLEY DOWN. A ridge in E. Devon some 10 miles north of the coast which separates the rivers Kit and Yarty. It is the location of the property called SELAH which is currently in private ownership and is not open to the public.

CHIRNSIDE 1
AUXILIARY UNITS
Special Duties Branch OUT-Station

by

Captain Hugh May, FRGS, Royal Navy

Contributing authors
A.S.G. Blackmore, D. Hunt, T.R.N. Walford

Foreword by
Admiral Sir Nigel Essenhigh, GCB

Copyright © 2014 by H.P. May.

First published in this form in Great Britain in 2014
by Dudfield Publications,
Green Down House, Green Down,
Axminster, Devon EX13 7TD

All rights reserved. No part of this publication
may be reproduced, stored in a retrieval system
or transmitted, in any form or by any means,
electronic, mechanical, photocopying, recording
or otherwise, without the prior consent in writing
of Dudfield Publications.

1st Impression: 2014

Printed and bound in Great Britain by Creeds, Bridport, Dorset

ISBN: 978-0-9929139-0-8

"On the British the threat of invasion had a more vivid, direct and comprehensive impact, for the danger, and the precautions taken to avert it, affected the whole population. Yet legend plays a large part in their memories of that tense and strangely exhilarating summer, and their experiences, like those of early childhood, are sharply rather than accurately etched upon their minds. The stories they tell of the period have become better, but not more veracious, with the passage of time. Rumours are remembered as facts, and – particularly since anti-invasion precautions continued in force for several years after the Germans had renounced their project – the sequence of events is blurred."

Peter Fleming

(Captain Peter Fleming, founder Kent Auxiliary Units 1940)

DEDICATED

TO THE MEMORY OF

MY GRANDUNCLES

Peter Langton May and Frederick Sturdy May

who together with their brother-in-law

Leonard William Lamaison

gave their lives for their country

1914 – 1918

Contents

			Page
	Acknowledgements		*viii*
	Foreword		*ix*
	Preface		*xi*
1	GHQ Auxiliary Units	– David Hunt	1
2	The Property	– Hugh May	16
3	Arthur Douglas Ingrams and family	– Hugh May	20
4	Construction	– Stanley Blackmore	31
5	The Wireless and Electrical installation	– Tim Walford	74
	Postscript		98

ANNEX

A	Drawings	99
B	CHIRNSIDE 1 Timeline	110
	Abbreviations and Glossary	111
	Selected bibliography and data source	118
	Index	119

Acknowledgements

The assistance given to me throughout this project has come from many individuals and a wide variety of sources. Without those members of the project team who have given so generously their time and expertise little would have been achieved. Not only has the restoration programme, which involved many hours of practical work, been largely completed but also the compilation and documentation of our findings which has resulted in this publication. To my fellow project team members – Stanley Blackmore, David Hunt and Tim Walford – a most sincere 'thank you.'

I am particularly grateful to John Warwicker who has so willingly shared his unrivalled knowledge of Auxiliary Units with the project team, his encouragement and support have been a key factor in working with the pieces of the jig-saw. The following people have had an input to the project which is very much appreciated – Donald Brown, Richard Chapple, Barbara Culleton, Colin Guy, Andy Howgate, Corinne Miller, Parham Museum, Geoffrey Pidgeon, Chris Sennett, Vintage and Military Amateur Radio Society, Ken Ward, William Ward, Derrick Warren and Tim Wray. Editorial advice from Trisha Barbor, Robert and Penny Luther was invaluable.

Finally, my special thanks for the crucial assistance provided by Mrs David Ingrams which has been fundamental to the project. I have been given access to family records and papers relating to Douglas Ingrams, all of which have helped immeasurably in the understanding of the intricacies and secrecy surrounding the wartime activities of the Auxiliary Units Special Duties Branch, particularly those associated with SELAH.

Hugh May
2014

Foreword

In 1909 Captain Sir George Mansfield Smith-Cumming, Royal Navy was appointed as the first Director of the Secret Service Bureau. Admiral Sir Hugh Sinclair succeeded him in 1923 and remained in post until 1939. These two Royal Navy officers built the foundations on which the Secret Intelligence Service (MI6) and the Security Service (MI5) evolved. In the Second World War it was through these organisations that the concept of Irregular Warfare developed which led to the formation of Auxiliary Units.

On 8th August 2006, once again a Captain was followed by an Admiral, not this time in official appointments, but in an investigation of an Auxiliary Units Special Duties Branch dugout.

I followed Hugh May and descended 10 ft. underground by way of a vertical ladder bolted to a concrete wall. Together we entered a manmade chamber unlike anything I have previously encountered. Stooping low, we moved slowly along a short, dark passage that culminated in a lobby where there was space to stand upright and where we could take stock of our surroundings. We were in the Maproom of the dugout at SELAH. Confronting us was a wall made from old railway sleepers and in this was hidden the secret access to the Radio room. The access was slightly ajar, and curious to see what lay behind, we raised the baulks of timber and entry was made.

It is not known how many people might have entered this compartment since it ceased to be operational in 1944; almost certainly no one during the following 35 years while Douglas Ingrams continued living at SELAH and, subsequently, perhaps one or two people only. The secrecy that surrounded the Auxiliary Units Special Duties Branch whilst they were operational largely remains today. Project CHIRNSIDE has assembled a remarkable account of this clandestine organisation supported by firm factual evidence and diligent research.

The many intriguing aspects of the Special Duties Branch will continue to attract writers and historians and there will always be scope for further research particularly if/when further classified documents become available for public scrutiny. However, this account is an invaluable addition to the subject and provides an absorbing insight into a chapter of WWII history, the detail of which has, to date, remained largely unpublished.

Sir Nigel Essenhigh, GCB
First Sea Lord
2001 – 2002

Preface

The property, known as SELAH (Plate 1), was purchased by the May family at the end of 2005. The Estate Agent's particulars of the property contained a brief mention of a WWII Bunker being in the garden but gave no details. There was nothing particularly eye-catching about the two original back to back cottage privies under which the construction was said to exist, its existence had no influence at all in the decision to purchase the property (Plates 2-7).

After moving to the property in February 2006, several days passed before an opportunity arose to investigate further and discover exactly what constituted the Bunker. A look inside the north privy revealed nothing more than assorted flowerpots and other gardening effects, no fittings other than a toilet paper holder remained. The door to the south privy was padlocked and it was only some days later that a key marked 'Aux Unit' was found in the house and the door could be opened. From this point on the task of unravelling the story of the dugout has become a fascinating and absorbing project.

The existence of a highly classified clandestine wartime organisation known as Auxiliary Units (AU) is not in doubt. Some former members have been traced and a few official documents containing references to the organisation have come to light. There is every reason to believe that details of the organisation and its conduct of operations were recorded at the time. However to date, for whatever reason, such information is not available. The secrecy surrounding the organisation remains firmly in place.

Until the 1990's the existence of this dugout remained a very well kept secret closely guarded by the wartime owner of the property under the shield of the Official Secrets Act and the almost total embargo on the release of official details into the public domain.

The need to search for and acquire an understanding of AU became fundamental. Efforts to recount the history of the AU organisation have resulted in a few publications. The establishing of the British Resistance

Organisation Museum (BROM) in 1997 focused public interest on the subject and more recently in 2009 the Coleshill Auxiliary Research Team was established. Authors have been very limited in their source data even after extensive research. Without doubt there remain many questions to be answered, disclosed and unearthed, but when further revelations will come to light remains unknown and unpredictable.

The following account provides a detailed look at one unique piece of the AU jig-saw and is intended to complement existing research and publications. An outline of the AU organisation is included as essential background to an understanding of this East Devon site, and is not intended to be a comprehensive history of the organisation. The Bewley Down site is of particular historic merit and is arguably the most significant surviving example of its type in the country. The fact that this Special Duties Branch OUT-Station (Code name CHIRNSIDE 1) was established at the home of the Ingrams family and their continual ownership of the property from 1928 – 2001 has undoubtedly contributed to its survival.

It is intended that this manuscript will record and discuss a detailed examination of a vital and fundamental aspect of the Special Duties Branch – a surviving OUT-Station. Not only has there been the unique opportunity to survey and record what exists but also to restore and renovate some of the fabric and fittings which have decayed over the years. In addition further research has enabled some accepted aspects of the AU story to be challenged and alternative explanations suggested.

The conceived project of investigation and restoration clearly demanded a wide variety of skills. With this in mind, a Project Team was formed, was up and running by the beginning of 2008 and consisted of the following four persons:

Captain H.P. May, FRGS, RN	Owner and Project leader
A.S.G. Blackmore, JP, DA, FRIBA	Architect and former RE Surveyor
Colonel D. Hunt, OBE, CEng, MIET Royal Signals (Retd.)	Military Historian
T. R. N. Walford, BSc, MIET, CEng	Electronic Engineer

Preface

During the following two years much of the planned restoration and renovation was achieved. The site was surveyed and architectural plans drawn after many weeks of detailed examination involving discovery, conjecture and, at times, bafflement. It was inevitable that the project team were faced with the difficult task of recording a measured view when a paucity of factual evidence needed to be balanced against a wider opinion based on specialist experience. Previously available information about the site has not always proved correct and clarification of fact and fiction has been rigorously addressed. The Project remains ongoing. There are many aspects which require further research such as details of the personnel involved and the concept of operations as well as clarifying the fundamental issue of the radio communications equipment. The dugout is clearly non-standard and was built to particularly exacting requirements. If the requirement was simply to conceal a radio at SELAH, the variety of farm sheds and buildings could have provided cover and the house itself with a high large E – W orientated roof would have been suitable for the VHF aerial. The conversion of some attic space for the operating position would have been relatively simple.

Equally important is the uncertainty surrounding the role of Douglas Ingrams. Whilst there is no doubt regarding his role as a Special Duties Branch Intelligence Officer based at Taunton and later in Norfolk, it is suggested that he might well have been recruited by the Secret Intelligence Service (SIS) before the construction of the dugout in 1941 and quite possibly pre-war.

Unless further evidence comes to light in the future there will remain uncertainty regarding the precise role played by Douglas Ingrams and the site at Bewley Down. Many questions remain unanswered but hopefully historians and students of the subject will continue their research and in time more facts will be uncovered.

CHIRNSIDE 1

PRIVY SITE

2008

Plate 2

2008

Plate 3

Preface

PRIVY OUTBUILDING

2008

Plate 4

2008

Plate 5

CHIRNSIDE 1
PRIVY OUTBUILDING

Courtesy D. Warren *Circa 2001*
Plate 6

2009
Plate 7

1
GHQ Auxiliary Units

BACKGROUND

The local spy network Douglas Ingrams set up in East Devon was an integral part of the British spy ring established in 1940 on the instigation of the Prime Minister, Winston Churchill, in the event of German occupation of parts of Britain. The underground facility at Bewley Down was the centre of the East Devon spy network and was its link into the national spy ring.

After the evacuation of British Expeditionary Force (BEF) from Dunkirk and the remaining British forces in France by mid June 1940, the threat of German invasion increased, particularly since the French capitulation on 16 June gave German access to the whole of the French coast. In June 1940 Churchill and the Inner War Cabinet gave approval to the Army to set up an organisation named Auxiliary Units. An insignificant title deliberately chosen for a clandestine organisation whose origins were the outcome of a pre-war 'think tank' cell operating within the British Secret Services and Military Intelligence. The results of this interaction were proposals and plans which embraced entirely new concepts of warfare, which at the time, were most irregular but by today's standards have become routine and acceptable. They included the formation of Commando Units, Special Operations Executive and GHQ Auxiliary Units all under the concept of IRREGULAR WARFARE.

The title GHQ Auxiliary Units indicated that they were controlled from General Headquarters (GHQ) Home Forces, the highest Army command level in Britain below the War Office, yet it gave no indication of any geographical responsibilities or role. The word Auxiliary was frequently used at that time and a number of key organisations ranging from the Auxiliary Territorial Service (ATS) of uniformed women supporting the Army to the Auxiliary Air Force and the civilian Auxiliary Fire Service. The use of the plural 'units' gave no indication of the number of units involved; particularly at the time when GHQ Home Forces was being expanded to command evacuated BEF units and formations and to take on the role of defending Great Britain against invasion.

Headed by Colonel Colin McVean Gubbins, the highest levels of secrecy were accorded to AU whose original HQ was at 7 Whitehall Place, London, before moving to Coleshill House Wiltshire in August 1940. From this HQ, the Operational Branch was directed, administered and trained. Later GHQ Auxiliary Units became the home or possibly the 'front' for an organisation whose origins were within MI6; which is perhaps better known as the Secret Intelligence Service (SIS). This organisation was the Special Duties Branch of GHQ Auxiliary Units.

OPERATIONAL BRANCH

The Operational Branch involved the selection, recruitment, training and equipping of civilians to undertake an operational role that was illegal under international law. Their role after invasion was to remain in German occupied areas, to conceal themselves in hide-outs during the day and to emerge and attack the enemy by night. Major N V Oxenden in his 1944 Auxiliary Units History and Achievement states:

'Their mission was to create havoc and destruction among the enemy's supplies and communications.'

At the time, the term 'communications' referred to roads, railways, waterways, etc., and not to signalling and telecommunications which were referred to as 'intercommunication.'

The recruited personnel were organised in a structure which preserved anonymity and were initially designated as Observation Units. They were led by so called Intelligence Officers (IO), practical men with initiative and imagination who were their field commanders. About 12 of these IOs in the rank of Captain were appointed by July 1940 each with the mission of recruiting 30 reliable men to form their cells of fighting patrols. Initially consisting of 5 men they were later increased to 7. Originally these men were exclusively civilians, mainly from a Home Guard recruiting base which included WW1 veterans and those in reserved occupations such as farmers and farm workers, miners, quarrymen, foresters and estate workers. As members of the Home Guard they had military status which might possibly

GHQ AUX UNITS - OPERATIONAL BRANCH CHAIN OF COMMAND

- GHQ Home Forces
- HQ GHQ Auxiliary Units
  - Operational Branch
  - Special Duties Branch
- Local Army HQ
- Ops IOs
- Liaison
- Group Commanders
- Scout Sections
- Liaison
- Training
- Patrol Leaders in Operational Bases (OB)

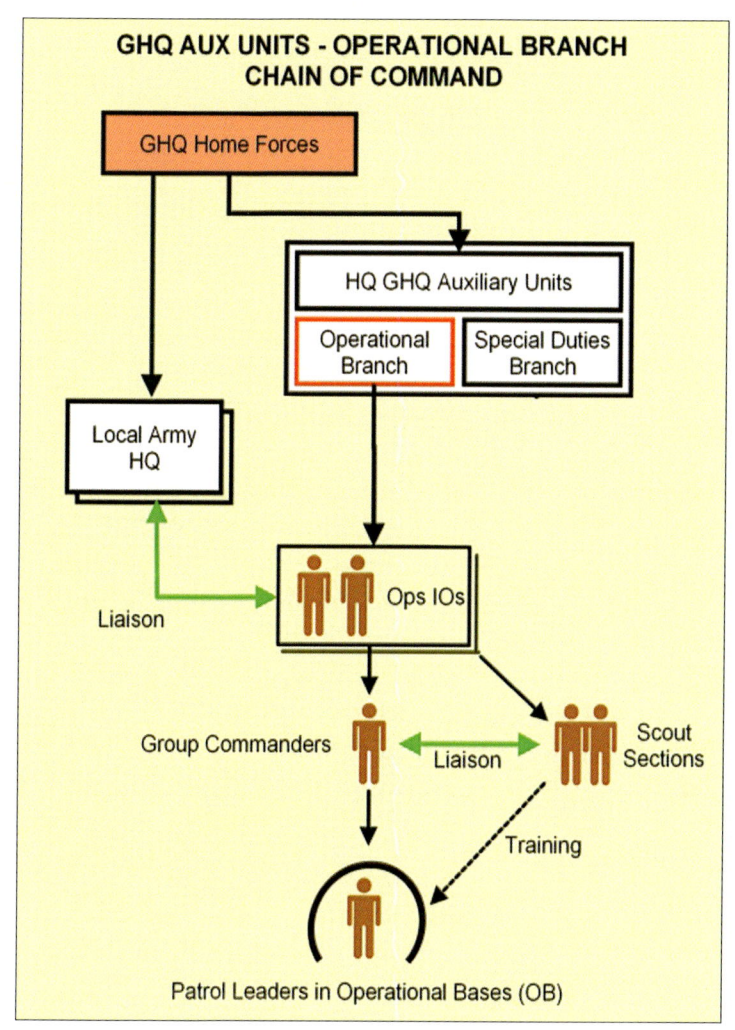

Plate 8

help if they were captured by the Germans. Group Commanders and Patrol Leaders were appointed within the structure while selected regular soldiers made up Scout Sections that provided training and instruction but also had an operational role (Plate 8).

Men of the Operational Branch, often known as 'auxiliers', were formed into Operational patrols. Colonel Gubbins reported that in the South West, work started on 16 July 1940 and by 26 July 1940 some 200 men had been enrolled and 115 dumps of arms and equipment established. Gubbins clearly stated: '...*the establishment does not permit the whole of the country to be covered.*' Despite popular assertions, the Operational Branch never attempted to cover the whole of the country, at best, the patrols covered less than 20% of Britain.

SPECIAL DUTIES BRANCH

The Special Duties Branch controlled a cadre of civilians who, after invasion, would remain in any occupied coastal area and gather intelligence about the invader. Unlike Operational patrols, it consisted of both men and women, who would carry on with their normal jobs, observe the Germans and send written reports via a chain of runners to the nearest Army HQ. These men and women of the Special Duties Organisation were quite simply spies although euphemistically referred to as Observers. When suitable wireless sets became available in 1941 or later, their role included manning hidden wireless stations to send intelligence out of enemy occupied areas.

Special Duties members operated on a cellular basis in complete isolation so that nobody knew who else was involved. They were even unknown to the Operational Branch. Within the Army, the existence of Special Duties Branch was classified as MOST SECRET and their role was only known to a few at the very highest level and then on a strict 'need to know' basis.

A contemporary document in the National Archives states:

> *'The SPECIAL DUTIES Branch of AUXILIARY UNITS is organised to provide information for military formations in the event of enemy invasion or raids in GREAT BRITAIN, from areas temporarily or permanently in enemy control. All this information would be collected as a result of direct observation by specially recruited and trained civilians who would remain in enemy occupied areas.'*

This description of their duties implies that they were not expected to steal maps and documents, and the phrase 'direct observation' would appear to eliminate the collecting of hearsay information or reports from third parties, which so often could be exaggerated and inaccurate. It also implies a degree of mobility to get out and about unseen within occupied areas.

In his report of 26 July 1940, the Commander of AU made no direct mention of the Special Duties Branch except the simple statement: *'The other role* [of AU] *is Intelligence.'*

The War Establishment (a vital document authorising manpower and resources) approved in August 1940 only included HQ staff (a commander with 5 staff officers, 11 intelligence officers, clerks, drivers and batmen). There were no signallers on this first Establishment, which strongly suggests that there were no Special Duties wireless networks in operation at this time, nor were there any immediate plans for their introduction. It was noted on 11 July 1940 that the Special Duties Branch had already been formed and that the War Establishment suggested by Colonel Gubbins had been approved by the Chief of General Staff at GHQ Home Forces. The Special Duties organisation was stated to have already *'commenced activities'*, It was *'attached to the HQ of Aux Units'* which suggests that at the time it belonged to some other organisation. GHQ Home Forces asked the War Office if the suggested Establishment could be passed through the War Establishments Committee without any further comment or discussion. This would have been a most rare occurrence for this powerful committee to retrospectively approve, 'on the nod', an organisation already formed and operating, particularly in the difficult days after Dunkirk when the Field Army was reorganising to meet an invasion and was desperately short of weapons, equipment and vehicles.

Until 1942 the HQ for the Special Duties Branch was located a few miles from Coleshill House at Hannington Hall. Major Maurice Petherick was the officer commanding Special Duties, and although nominally responsible to the Commander AU, he operated independently. Few details of Special Duties structure and operations are known. The scraps of information that have come to light raise the question of who was in the 'driving seat'. Was the new Special Duties Branch actually controlled by the Military or was it attached to the SIS who retained ultimate control?

Personnel

The Special Duties IOs were Army officers posted in with the rank of Captain, who recruited specially selected and vetted civilians as Key Men

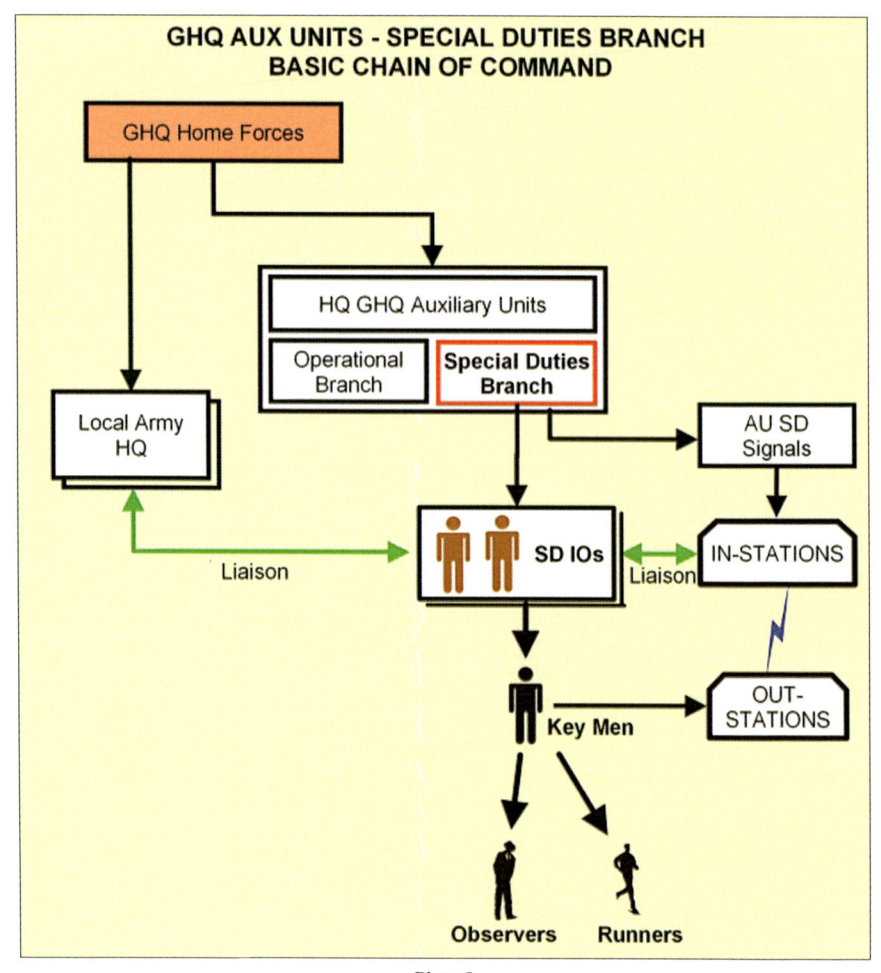

**GHQ AUX UNITS - SPECIAL DUTIES BRANCH
BASIC CHAIN OF COMMAND**

Plate 9

who each ran a local observer and runner network (Plate 9). The first AU Special Duties Establishment showed 11 IOs and the number never rose above 12, which suggests that the initial Special Duties coverage remained reasonably constant throughout the life of Special Duties.

The researcher and author John Warwicker writes that:

> 'Those in-the-field were selected from an index of names, carefully drawn up and vetted, some before the outbreak of hostilities, drawing upon the personal recommendation of an

Establishment inner circle connected by birth, or tradition, through Universities or the Armed Forces, Whitehall or prestigious London Clubs. Others came more locally from Regional Commissioner to Section 'D' recommendation.'

It is suggested that these were the Key Men who were chosen from this background, each being responsible for recruiting and training observers and runners. Douglas Ingrams was one of these Key Men initially, and the IO responsible for Somerset and Devon in 1940 was Captain Coxwell-Rogers.

The civilian observers were generally pre selected, vetted by the police and then asked to join. Unlike Operational patrols, the requirement was not for tough, outdoor types capable of hand to hand combat and trained in the use of arms and explosives. Amongst the essential qualifications were exemption from military service and the capability of unremarkable mobility within an area surrounding their place of work or home both before and after invasion. Doctors, clergymen, tradesmen, suppliers and retired Army personnel were likely candidates for recruitment as observers, while other civilians were taken on as runners.

Maintenance of the high level of secrecy accorded to the Special Duties Branch and its personnel was underpinned by rigorous application of the Official Secrets Act.

Areas of Deployment and Role

The Special Duties observer networks were only deployed in and near coastal areas where there was a threat of invasion. Little information on the extent of the Special Duties coverage has come to light and the only source of reliable information is a map of the wireless networks deployed by 1944, which clearly confirms the deployment in coastal areas only. Initially the wireless coverage was in Kent, Surrey and East Anglia but, as the war went on, there was a steady expansion northwards from The Wash and by 1944 had reached Midlothian, East Lothian, Fife and Angus together with further coverage along the Sutherland and Caithness coast. The wireless coverage also expanded westwards along the South Coast from Hampshire through Dorset and East Devon with further deployment in south and west Somerset. Lastly coverage was also provided for the South Wales coast

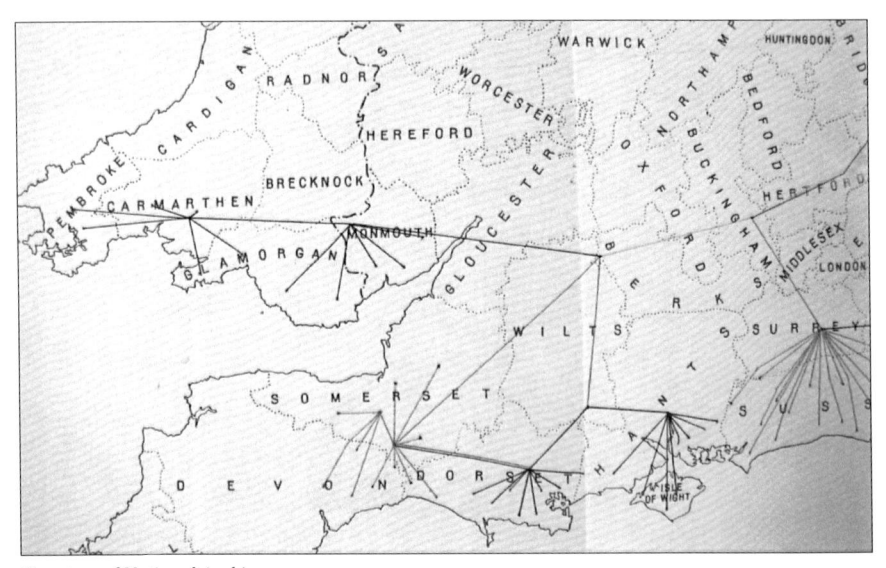

Courtesy of National Archives
AU Special Duties wireless networks (July 1944)
Plate 10

(Plate 10). At the centre of each network is an IN-Station with radial links to the OUT-Stations.

Once recruited, observers would be instructed in the recognition of enemy forces and briefed as to the intelligence required by their IO. Reports would be left in pre arranged dead letter drops then collected by a runner who was trained to covertly deliver the report to the next drop and so on. Plate 11 shows a demonstration dead letter drop, a metal field gate hook where a message was left in a vertical hole bored into the base. This example is one of several used by Douglas Ingrams for training purposes and was presented to The British Resistance Organisation museum at Parham by his son David.

This chain of runners delivering to and picking up messages from dead letter drops ensured that tight security would be maintained regarding the identity of observers, runners and the locations to which the messages were being delivered. The only exception appears to have been the Key Man, who having recruited and trained his team must have known them all. This presented the obvious danger that if any team member gave the IO's name to the enemy under duress, the enemy would have immediately searched in and

Dead Letter Drop
Plate 11

around the IO's home. This may be the reason why the dugout at SELAH, which was said by Douglas Ingram's son, David, to have been built in the spring of 1941, was built more than a year before the wireless networks were extended into Somerset and East Devon. The dugout could have been originally intended to give him protection from searching Germans.

As the threat of invasion diminished, the possibility of raids against key vulnerable points was identified. Oxenden (1944) writes:

> 'In the early summer of 1942 the Home Guard was warned that local raids might be expected upon our priority coasts, and all units work out their lead roles. This warning was a gift to IOs, for although no universally applicable directive could be issued from HQ, they were able to formulate their own in conjunction with their own local military commander.'

The Special Duties organisation adapted to this new role and trained to collect intelligence about the movement of raiders and pass it on to both the

Army and also to the local Operational patrols. Raiders might land from the sea or by parachute but it was considered that they would then be recovered by sea. The Operational patrol's role was to attempt to cut off the raiders as they withdrew to the beaches.

As D-Day approached, the Special Duties organisation took on another role in the areas where the build up for the invasion was taking place. They were tasked with listening into conversations and reporting the views of the civilian population about where and when the invasion might be launched. Wireless stations were manned on a 24-hour basis. In his farewell letter to the Special Duties civilian personnel the Commander in Chief of Home Forces, General Franklyn, wrote:

> *'In recent days while our invasion forces were concentrating, an additional heavy burden was placed on those of you responsible for the maintenance of good security, to ensure that the enemy was denied foreknowledge of our plans and preparations. The Security Reports regularly provided by Special Duties have proved of invaluable assistance to our security staffs.'*

Communications

Before wireless was deployed, communications across the front line from out of the occupied area relied on local solutions. Whilst referring to the Operational Branch in particular, Oxenden (1944) provides details of such solutions.

> *'IOs were urged to experiment with messenger dogs, carrier pigeons, light signals flashed down carefully aimed pipes, call-boxes, and even relay teams mounted on horses and avoiding the roads. One IO managed to send a message across his county, through a team of seven riders, at speeds that were considered very creditable...'*

There is evidence of messages being taken by pony from the home of a Key Man in the Vale of Marshwood (to the east of Bewley Down) in Dorset, eastwards to an unknown farm at an inland location. It should be noted that the military HQ responsible for Dorset was located to the east at Blandford Forum. Mention of call-boxes suggests the use of the GPO public telephone network but lines into occupied areas would have been cut off as part of the military denial measures to prevent the invader from communicating to agents outside the occupied areas.

Although the Special Duties Branch was clearly formed in July 1940, the provision of wireless communications, with some notable exceptions in Kent, commenced in early 1941. Wireless networks for East Devon and Somerset were authorised on 30 March 1942. Implementation began with the posting in of Royal Signals tradesmen and the establishment of the AU Signals organisation at Bachelor's Hall at Hundon in Suffolk under Captain Hills and his second in command Captain Ken Ward.

The role of AU Signals was *'to provide the communications to enable the civilian observers to pass their information to a military HQ.'* This implies communicating from within the occupied area across the front line to a military HQ (Plate 12).

The basic wireless system consisted of concealed OUT-Stations mainly in the coastal belt equipped with a special wireless set providing radio telephony communications to military manned IN-Stations sited well inland from the coast. Each observer network had an OUT-Station which was run by the Key Man responsible for the observers and runners. All these were

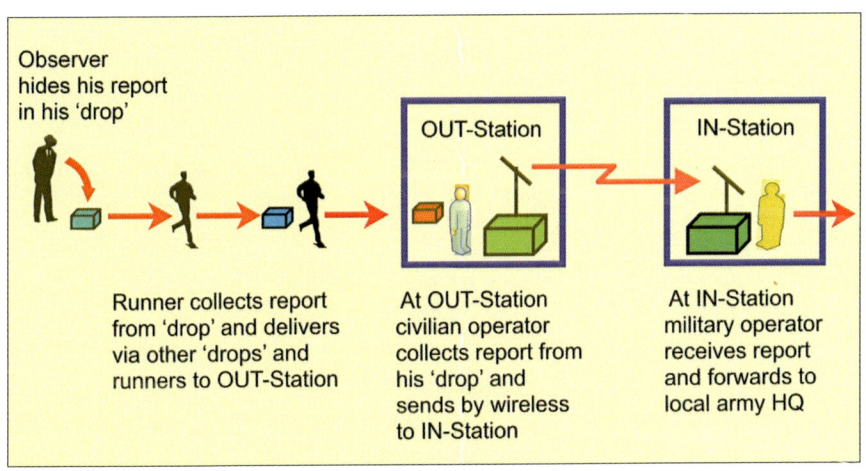

Basic AU Special Duties Organisation
Plate 12

concealed, with many in underground dugouts similar to the installation at SELAH. They were equipped to function should the area in which they were situated be occupied by the enemy. Most OUT-Stations appear to have been within approximately 5 miles of the coast.

At the OUT-Station, the Key Man or his civilian operator would transmit reports to the IN-Station, which would forward it by various means to the Army HQ responsible for the area. In the case of east Devon, this was HQ 8th Corps (from 1943 HQ South Western District) at Pyrland Hall 2 miles to the north of Taunton.

The 1941 AU Signals Establishment included 40 officers of the ATS to man some of the IN-Stations. These officers also trained civilian OUT-Station operators. Two ATS signals officers, Mary Alexander and Priscilla Badgerow are known to have visited SELAH.

An extract from the Ingrams family visitors' book for 1943 confirms one of their visits with added comment (green ink) by Douglas Ingrams (Plate 13).

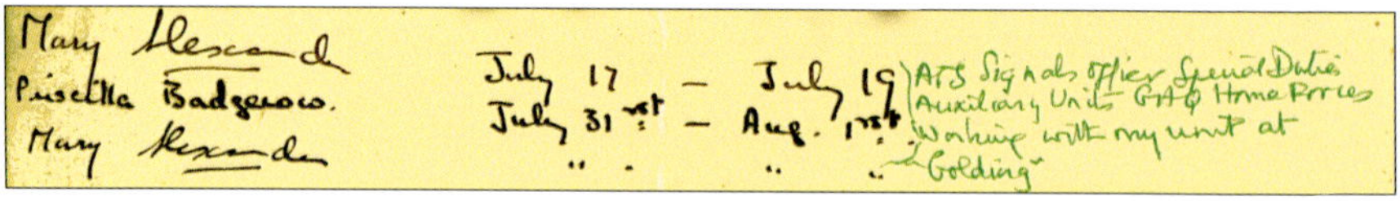
Mary Alexander July 17 – July 19 ATS Signals Officer Special Duties Auxiliary Units GHQ Home Forces Working with my unit at "Golding"
Priscilla Badgerow July 31st – Aug. 1st
Mary Alexander " " " "

Visitors' Book (extract)
Plate 13

When wireless became available in east Devon in 1942, the dugout at SELAH became an OUT-Station (CHIRNSIDE 1) on the CHIRNSIDE wireless network with the CONTROL or IN-Station situated 7 miles to the north at Castle Neroche near Buckland St Mary and 8 miles south of HQ 8th. Corps, which CHIRNSIDE 0 served. CHIRNSIDE 0 could relay messages to Pyrland Hall by GPO telephone or another wireless link to a station called GOLDING some 9 miles to the north and about 1 mile NE of the HQ on the edge of the Quantock Hills.

Plate 14 shows the basic wireless network configuration, which used the specially designed TRD wireless sets. By July 1944 there were some 125 OUT-Stations working to 30 IN-Stations.

In 1943 some 78 of the OUT-Stations were provided with wireless links to a SUB-OUT-Station giving a second point within their areas of

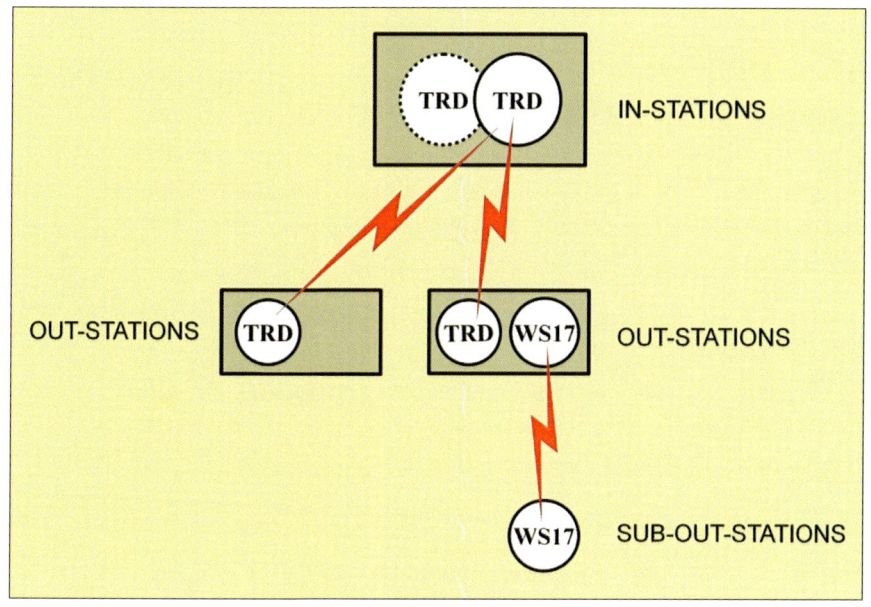

Basic Network Configuration
Plate 14

responsibility where reports could be sent by wireless with minimum delay to the OUT-Station for onward transmission. These used the Wireless Set 17 (WS17). CHIRNSIDE 1 at Bewley Down had a SUB-OUT-Station hidden in an attic in the small town of Axminster some 4 miles away towards the coast.

Royal Signals technicians made regular discrete visits to all OUT-Station sites to maintain the wireless sets and the concealed aerials, which were often slung high up in nearby trees. They also exchanged the wireless batteries in use for fully charged batteries. It took a lot of cunning to enter and leave a site or to work on a tree aerial without being seen by local people.

It is recorded that the Special Duties Branch employed 3250 civilians as observers, runners and operators who manned the OUT-Stations and SUB-OUT-Stations. These figures suggest that, on average, about 26 civilians worked within the area served by each OUT-Station.

Disbandment

On the 4 July 1944 a letter from General Franklyn, the General Officer Command-in-Chief (GOC-in-C) Home Forces, to Colonel Douglas announced that: '...*it is no longer possible to retain the Special Duties organisation...*' With the diminished risk of invasion and enemy raids there was a more pressing demand for the redeployment of military personnel elsewhere. General Franklyn went on to state:

> '*This organisation founded on the keenness and patriotism of selected civilians of all grades, has been in a position through the constant and thorough training to furnish accurate information on raids or invasion instantly to military headquarters throughout the country.*'

Due to the highly classified nature of the organisation:

> '*...no public recognition can be given for this job, it is my wish that a copy of this letter be sent to all members of the Special Duties organisation as my acknowledgement of the value and efficiency of their work.*'

But sadly, after the war, the Honours Committee ruled that the civilian Special Duties Branch observers, runners and key men were not eligible for the Defence Medal; although the auxiliers of the Operational Branch, who were enrolled into the Home Guard and who had served for the requisite period of three years, were eventually allowed to claim the medal. They were not alone, as other civilians, for example technicians working on AA gun sites, and women members of the Home Guard were also refused the medal. A rather cutting remark on a War Office file minute dated 4 November 1948 from the Director of Personnel Services (Army) to the Military Secretary, which was passed through the Director of Military Intelligence considered that:

> '*...the decision of the* [Honours] *Committee was the only one that they could reach. The over-riding consideration surely is that in the event the direct contribution of these people to the defence of the UK was nil. It is difficult to give them a medal for what they might have done if an invasion had occurred.*'

Following the decision not *'to retain'* the organisation, measures to destroy the evidence were implemented. Wireless sets were collected, passed to 1 SCU (Special Communications Unit) and later destroyed. A paper dated 1944 in the National Archives stresses the importance of closing down and destroying the AU facilities to prevent auxiliers from boasting about their escapades and showing off their Operational base sites, but more important, to prevent construction and access methods getting into the public domain as the techniques might be needed in the future. This included Special Duties dugouts and it was suggested by Commander Auxiliary Units that Special Duties dugouts would have to be dealt with by regular personnel.

AU sites can be grouped into three categories. Those built on requisitioned land, others built secretly without the landowner's knowledge and those on land belonging to AU members. The first two categories would have required greater effort to close down than the third as AU members could continue to exercise security. A progress report on the close down of AU dated 17 August 1944 reported that in all areas IN and OUT-Stations

> '...had been dismantled and closed down. All dugouts had been blocked as ordered by HQ Auxiliary Units...'

CHIRNSIDE 1 at Bewley Down was an OUT-Station in the Special Duties Branch wireless network and provides a unique insight into the role and structure of that clandestine organisation (ANNEX B). The fact that it has survived largely intact is remarkable and begs the question – Why? Was it an oversight, perhaps due to a lack of supervision and prioritisation by IOs? Or maybe deliberate?

2
The Property

The house on Bewley Down is believed to have been built during the late 19th. Century by a local man 'Dickie' Deane for his retirement from a seafaring career. The site (ANNEX A-1, A-2) commands arguably one of the finest panoramic views across East Devon. Facing south at a height of 218m the property looks across the Yarty valley and to the coast at Seaton where the sea horizon can often be seen. To the east the rolling hills of West Dorset punctuate the skyline and to the north open fields of Somerset provide a backdrop. The nearest neighbouring property is a farm 600m to the south. In 1910 the house, then known as SELAH VILLA (later known as SELAH COTTAGE or SELAH) was sold together with 12 acres of land (Plate 15).

1910

Auction
Plate 15

The Property

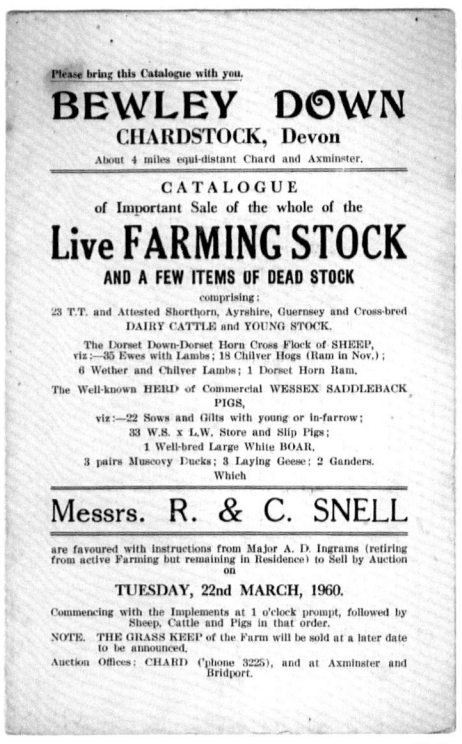

```
Please bring this Catalogue with you.
BEWLEY DOWN
CHARDSTOCK, Devon
About 4 miles equi-distant Chard and Axminster.

CATALOGUE
of Important Sale of the whole of the
Live FARMING STOCK
AND A FEW ITEMS OF DEAD STOCK
comprising:
23 T.T. and Attested Shorthorn, Ayrshire, Guernsey and Cross-bred
DAIRY CATTLE and YOUNG STOCK.
The Dorset Down-Dorset Horn Cross Flock of SHEEP,
viz:—35 Ewes with Lambs; 18 Chilver Hogs (Ram in Nov.);
6 Wether and Chilver Lambs; 1 Dorset Horn Ram.
The Well-known HERD of Commercial WESSEX SADDLEBACK
PIGS,
viz:—22 Sows and Gilts with young or in-farrow;
33 W.S. x L.W. Store and Slip Pigs;
1 Well-bred Large White BOAR.
3 pairs Muscovy Ducks; 3 Laying Geese; 2 Ganders.
Which

Messrs. R. & C. SNELL
are favoured with instructions from Major A. D. Ingrams (retiring
from active Farming but remaining in Residence) to Sell by Auction
on
TUESDAY, 22nd MARCH, 1960.
Commencing with the Implements at 1 o'clock prompt, followed by
Sheep, Cattle and Pigs in that order.
NOTE. THE GRASS KEEP of the Farm will be sold at a later date
to be announced.
Auction Offices: CHARD ('phone 3225), and at Axminster and
Bridport.
```

Courtesy J. Rowe   *1960*
Plate 16

In 1928 the property was occupied by a Miss Florence Moulton-Barrett whose reputation as a recluse was borne out by her obituary in the local newspaper… *'who spent her life and large inheritance befriending tramps, waifs, down and outs and dogs'*. The property was purchased by Douglas Ingrams in November of that year and remained within his family for the next 72 years. The two cottages were made into one family house which for many years was run as a small holding. In 1960 Douglas Ingrams retired and a farm sale of the livestock and machinery was held on site (Plate 16).

After Douglas' death in 1988, SELAH passed to his son David whose death in 2000 resulted in the property being put on the open market. During the intervening five years before the May family acquired the property, the house, garden and outbuildings were subjected to far reaching redevelopment. Fortunately the dugout remained largely unscathed and only suffered minor irreparable damage (Plates 17-20).

CHIRNSIDE 1

SELAH – NORTH ASPECT

G. Newbery collection   *1952*
Plate 17

2009
Plate 18

The Property

SELAH – SOUTH ASPECT

G. Newbery collection   1952
Plate 19

2007
Plate 20

3
Arthur Douglas Ingrams and Family

Arthur Douglas Ingrams was born in 1903, the youngest of three sons of the Reverend William Smith Ingrams, Housemaster at Shrewsbury School. He was commissioned in the Territorial Army (TA) in April 1923. (2nd. Lt. 60th/6th Cheshire & Shropshire Medium Brigade, Royal Garrison Artillery) and two years later joined the Colonial Office (Agriculture and Forestry Department) for service in Zanzibar Protectorate. He was joined there by his fiancée Eileen Shortt on 25th. February 1926 and they were married the following day. Eileen was one of three daughters of Sir Edward Shortt, former Chief Secretary for Ireland (1918-1919) and Home Secretary (1919-1922).

By mid 1927 Douglas and Eileen had returned to England briefly living in Kent before moving to Bewley Down. Three children were born to Douglas and Eileen, a son who died in infancy followed by a daughter Eileen Patricia born 1928 and a son David Douglas in 1930, both were raised at SELAH.

Douglas pursued his career as a farmer and played an active role in the Special Constabulary of the Devon Police rising to become Assistant Divisional Commandant in 1958 (Plate 21).

Whilst Douglas remained firmly attached to his Devon smallholding, his two older brothers had chosen very different careers. Harold, the eldest, became a highly respected and influential diplomat with the British Colonial Service, noted particularly for his work in Southern Arabia, where together with his (second) wife Doreen (née Shortt, sister of Douglas' wife Eileen) they significantly influenced the development of the Yemen and its inhabitants. They were awarded the prestigious Royal Geographical Society Gold Medal in 1940.

Leonard, his older brother led a most successful career in the banking industry, being known as 'The Flying Banker' due to his habit of piloting himself around Europe in his private Puss Moth plane on his business trips for the Chemical Bank of New York. It is known that Leonard had links

AD Ingrams with Devon 'Specials'
Plate 21

with MI6 and recruited journalist Sefton Delmer to the Political Warfare Executive (PWE). He was also implicated in a plot to assassinate Himmler and is thought to have been closely involved in the mystery of the flight of Rudolf Hess to Scotland. Not surprising that Leonard is listed on the Gestapo arrest list for Great Britain. The possibility that both Harold and Leonard had a significant influence on their brother's wartime service cannot be ignored.

There is no doubt that Douglas became an Special Duties Branch Key Man, exactly when and how he took on the role is not known, although sometime in 1940 is suggested. There are however indications that he may have been involved, as early as 1938, with earlier Resistance and Intelligence organisations namely Section D of MI6 (Home Defence Organisation) or MI(R) under Lt. Col Holland and Major Gubbins.

Little is known of Douglas's wartime activities other than he was most likely recruited into Special Duties by Captain Cecil Coxwell-Rogers

Captain AD Ingrams with Staff car and driver c1943 (Unconfirmed)
Plate 22

(whom he succeeded as IO in late 1943) (Plate 22). Douglas records that Coxwell-Rogers *'became a great friend of Eileen and me.'*

By Feb/Mar 1944, Douglas was relieved by Captain E.C.Grover and was appointed Special Duties Branch IO in Norfolk, replacing Major John Collings. His duties in the eastern part of the country required the approval and support of the local constabulary for which he was issued with the East Suffolk, Essex and Norfolk police passes (Plate 23).

On 21 April 1944, Douglas was issued with a new military identity card (Plate 24). Was this a replacement for a lost/damaged card or perhaps a new issue in preparation for a future assignment?

In the summer of 1944 the War Office reviewed the requirement for the Special Duties Branch, and after the Commander-in-Chief Home Forces, General Franklyn, wrote that it was *'no longer possible to retain the Special Duties Organisation'*, it became far from clear exactly what happened to the organisation and personnel. Were the 'Intelligence' skills of the Special Duties Branch redeployed or perhaps absorbed into other Security Organisations? Immediately post war, Douglas did not return to East Devon for any length of time, as might have been expected, but was reassigned to an unknown role within the Military.

Arthur Douglas Ingrams and Family

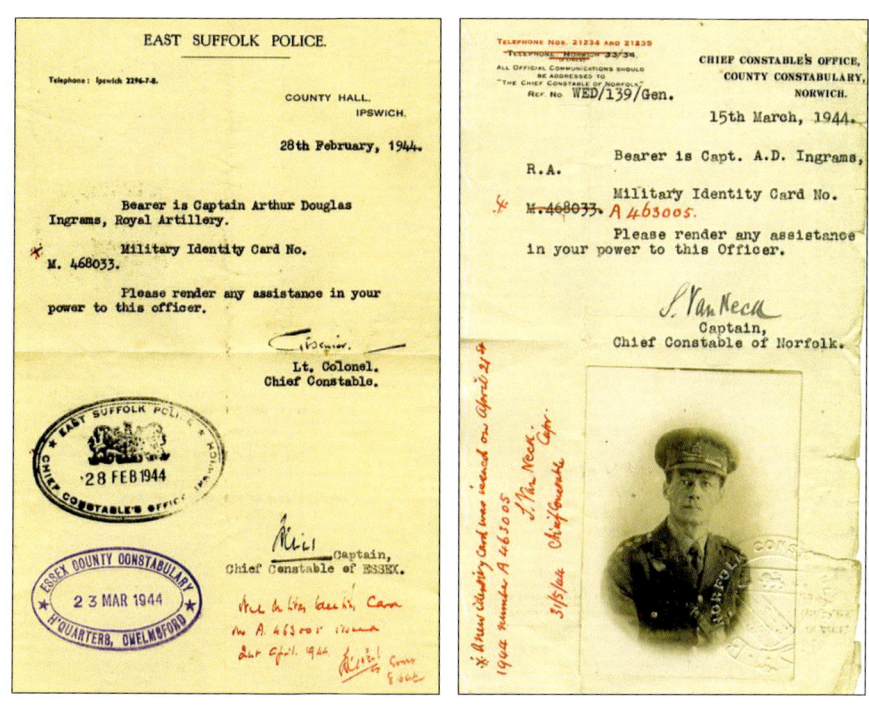

Police Passes issued Feb/Mar 1944
Plate 23

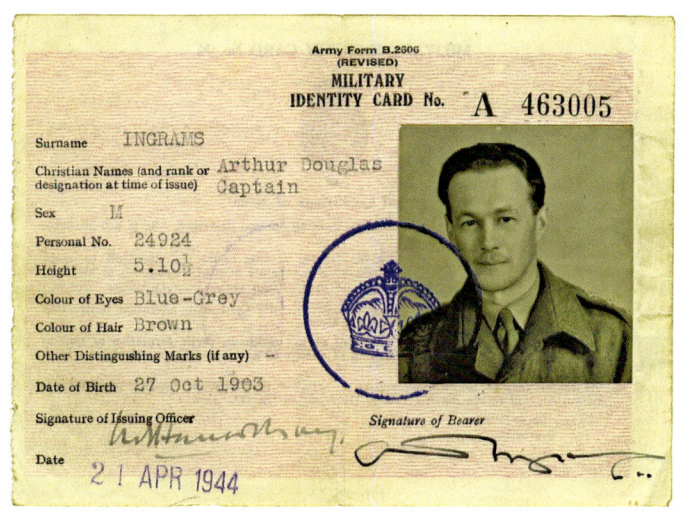

Military Identity Card issued Apr. 1944
Plate 24

Nine months after VE. Day, Douglas was known to be on Service in the Middle East in an unknown capacity but one that brought him into close contact with Saudi Royalty, close enough to be presented with a wrist watch

Presentation Wristwatch
Plate 25

by King Faisal dated 17 Feb 1946 (Plates 25, 26).

Five months later Douglas was in Egypt in the rank of Major for what purpose is unclear. Surviving memorabilia (Plates 27-29) in the possession

Saudi Royalty and Captain AD Ingrams (unconfirmed)
Plate 26

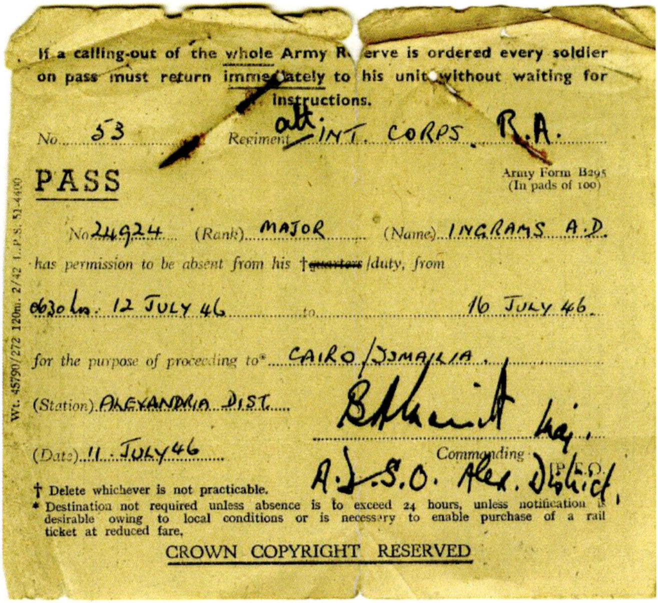
If a calling-out of the whole Army Reserve is ordered every soldier on pass must return immediately to his unit without waiting for instructions.

No. 53 Regiment att. INT. CORPS. R.A.

PASS

Army Form B295 (In pads of 100)

Wt. 45790/272 120m. 2/42 L.P.S. 51-4400

No. 24924 (Rank) MAJOR (Name) INGRAMS A.D.

has permission to be absent from his †quarters/duty, from

0630 hrs. 12 JULY 46 to 16 JULY 46.

for the purpose of proceeding to* CAIRO/ISMAILIA.

(Station) ALEXANDRIA DIST.

(Date) 11. JULY 46

Commanding

A.I.S.O. Alex. District

† Delete whichever is not practicable.

* Destination not required unless absence is to exceed 24 hours, unless notification is desirable owing to local conditions or is necessary to enable purchase of a rail ticket at reduced fare.

CROWN COPYRIGHT RESERVED

Alexandria District Military Pass
Plate 27

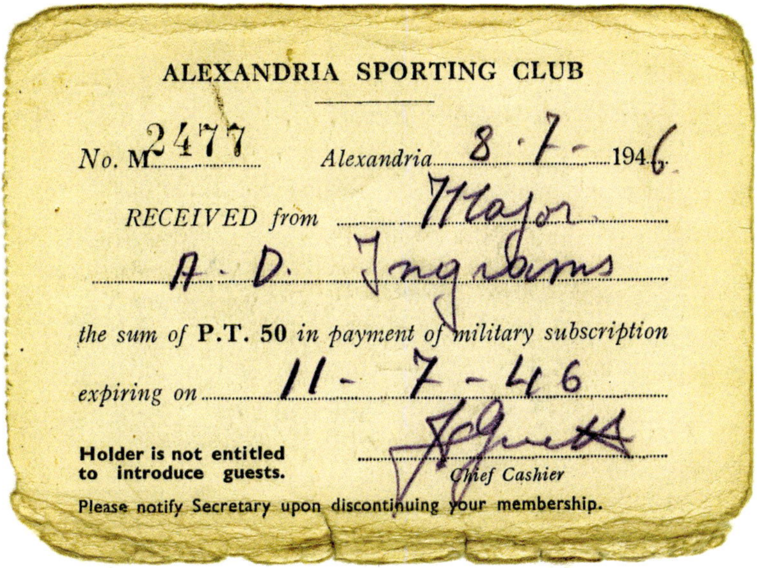
ALEXANDRIA SPORTING CLUB

No. M 2477 *Alexandria* 8·7· 1946

RECEIVED from Major A. D. Ingrams

the sum of **P.T. 50** *in payment of military subscription*

expiring on 11-7-46

Holder is not entitled to introduce guests.

Chief Cashier

Please notify Secretary upon discontinuing your membership.

Club subscription receipt
Plate 28

Major Ingrams with unidentified group (unconfirmed)
Plate 29

of the Ingrams family provide evidence of his visit but no detail.

The date Douglas returned to UK is not known nor is it certain when his military service terminated. However, from the 1950's Douglas and his wife continued living on Bewley Down. Eileen died in 1973. After remarriage in 1980, Douglas moved across the valley to live in the hamlet of Furley. He died at Chard Hospital on 16th. April 1988 (Plate 30).

David Ingrams was educated in England and subsequently spent much of his life in the United States of America choosing a career in Financial Services. Although he recalls his memories of the dugout being built and the secrecy impressed upon him by his father, it seems most likely that the subject was never discussed between them, either during or after the war.

MEMBURY MAN IS MOURNED

A MEMBURY man who was responsible for Winston Churchill's safety at the Big Three conference in Cairo during the Second World War was mourned by villagers last week.

Major Douglas Ingrams (85), who died in Chard Hospital, had been active in village affairs after coming to farm locally more than 60 years ago.

He was a former commandant of the Special Constabulary for Axminster and District and later for Honiton and district.

Maj Ingrams was born in Shrewsbury in 1903. He worked for some time on farms before going for forestry training. He entered the colonial service and was trained in more specialised .forestry work. His special 'work was on the island of Pemba, North Zanzibar. Ill-health forced him to return to England.

After working in the New Forest he and his wife decided to find a farm in the West and they bought Selah on Bewley Down in 1928. A few years ago he moved to Martins Cottage Furley, and handed the farm over to his son.

Before the war he became commandant of the Special Constabulary of Axminster district and during the war he worked for the information services in GHQ,

eventually working in the Middle East. It was while there that he was responsible for the security when Winston Churchill met King Ibn Saud outside Cairo. After the war he became commandant of the Honiton and district Special Constabulary.

He took an active part with his wife in village affairs at Membury for almost 60 years. He was a member of the parochial church council and was a supporter of plans to build a new village hall. He leaves a son and daughter, nine grandchildren and 10 great-grandchildren.

Courtesy ARCHANT

Plate 30

The wartime activities of his father were highly classified and they remain as such.

It wasn't until after his father's death and his return to Bewley Down that David began to take an interest and research the subject. *'My father was an Aux Unit IO here – sadly my interest developed only long after his death – so I had some reconstructing to do when the local History Society asked me to give a talk...'*

Secrecy is synonymous with AU, likewise knowledge of the Bewley Down site remained largely undisclosed for some 50 years. Other than members of the Ingrams family very few people, postwar, knew of its existence, one neighbour recalls being told about the site in 1973 by Douglas Ingrams, and that he was the first person Douglas had ever informed. Another neighbour who clearly remembers the war years in the area has stated that she had no knowledge whatsoever of operations at SELAH. Amazingly, a lady, Myrtle Moore (later Eames), working and living during the war at SELAH as a member of the Women's Land Army, made the same statement – she was not aware of the OUT-Station or any associated activity. Locally, it is suggested that Medora Eames of Woonton Farm, Chardstock assisted Douglas, but no details are known.

For the last five years of his life David was very much involved in obtaining official recognition by the Ministry of Defence of AU personnel and their entitlement to the Defence Medal. He concentrated on those from Devon, Somerset and Cornwall. At much the same time the Defence of Britain Project (1995 – 2002) was underway and the site and condition were recorded on a national database after field visits in 1997 and 98. The local Press reported the 'discovery' in February 1997 and printed photographs of David Ingrams and the privy (Plates 31-33).

A report written by author John Warwicker for the British Resistance Organisation museum (BRO) after his visit to Devon in 1999 records his meeting with David Ingrams. A brief description was written by Derrick Warren for the Somerset Industrial Archaeological Society and published in 2000. These various publications are believed to be the very first public acknowledgement of the existence of the dugout. They are all surprisingly limited with little comment on the operational aspects, this is not considered a failing, but further evidence of the secrecy that prevails.

● CONCEALED: The passage down to the wartime bunker beneath Mr Ingrams' privy

Secret wartime bunker hides wanted history

AN OUTSIDE toilet could hold the answer to some of the best-kept secrets of the Second World-War. For the privy in David Ingrams' garden on Bewley Down, Axminster, doubled as a top-secret bunker.

A concealed passage led ten feet underground to a top-security map room and radio room.

The chamber was built in 1941 as a vital nerve-centre for auxiliary units. It was a knee-jerk reaction in the event of Nazi invasion of Britain.

Spies, such as postmen and vets, were to collect information about the Germans to pass on to the British resistance. And 56 years later the bunker's radio wires, embedded in fir trees above ground, are still visible.

"In the opinion of the Defence of Britain project, this is one of the few remaining hide-outs and should be preserved," said Mr Ingrams, a 66-year-old retired financial services officer.

The bunker was built by sappers for his father, Major Douglas Ingrams, who led war-time territorial and special police forces in the area. "These men were later dropped overseas to teach people to run underground movements in other occupied countries."

Mr Ingrams (01404 881223) is appealing for people who served in wartime auxiliary units to tell him about their experiences, which information he can pass to the Imperial War Museum.

But so far some have asked him if it's all right to do so. "The culture of secrecy is very deeply ingrained. They were the first people to be recruited for secret operations," he added.

● HISTORY INSIDE: David Ingrams approaches the toilet in his Axminster garden

Courtesy Western Morning News

Plate 31

Loo leads to top-security bunker

SECRET BUNKER: David Ingrams in the Second World War bunker, under the outside loo, pictured below, at his home.

Privy to wartime secrets

AN OUTSIDE toilet could hold the answer to some of the best-kept secrets of the Second World War.

For the privy in David Ingrams' garden at Bewley Down, Axminster, doubled as a top-secret bunker.

A concealed passage led 10 feet underground to a top-security map room and radio room.

The chamber was built in 1941 as a vital nerve centre for auxiliary units in the event of a Nazi invasion.

Spies like postmen and vets were to collect information about the Germans to pass on to the British resistance. And 56 years later the bunker's radio wires embedded in fir trees are still visible.

"In the opinion of the Defence of Britain project this is one of the few remaining hide-outs and should be preserved," said Mr Ingrams, a 66-year-old retired financial services officer.

The bunker was built by sappers for his father, Major Douglas Ingrams, who led wartime territorial and special police forces in the area.

"Most other hide-outs were blown up to stop children or tractors falling into them," Mr Ingrams added.

Now he is appealing for people who served in wartime auxiliary units to tell him about their experiences.

He will pass the information on to the Imperial War Museum. Those he has managed to speak to so far have been very cagey.

Mr Ingrams said: "I have had three people recently say to me 'are you sure it's all right to talk'.

"The culture of secrecy is very deeply ingrained. They were the first people to be recruited for secret operations after the war."

☎ To get in touch with Mr Ingrams please call him on 01404 881223.

Courtesy ARCHANT

Plate 32

CHIRNSIDE 1

Toilet flushes best kept war secrets

AN OUTSIDE toilet in Membury has flushed some of the best kept secrets of the Second World War out into the open.

The toilet, which sits in David Ingram's garden, may look like an ordinary privy but beneath the floor lies a bunker complete with radio and map rooms.

Built in 1941 by Royal Engineer sappers, the bunker served as a centre for underground operations until the end of the war.

Radio and communications equipment was housed in the bunker and operated by auxiliary units specialising in top secret work. The radio wires still remain visible today.

Three soldiers worked eight hour shifts in the bunker which was only big enough for two plus a ventilation system.

Mr Ingram was 12 at the time the bunker was built and knew little about its importance.

He said: "I came home from prep school in the Easter holidays and I saw these soldiers digging a hole. When I came back in the summer holidays it was all done."

He added: "You would never have known."

He was sworn to secrecy by his father who served as a Major during the war and never mentioned the bunker to anyone until he married.

Now the bunker has attracted the attention of the Defence of Britain project which is trying to compile a database of hidden defences from around the country.

The bunker has been visited by representatives from the project who believe it is unlike anything they have ever seen.

Mr Ingram is now trying to contact people who served in auxiliary units so that he can learn about their experiences. Any information he gets he hopes to pass on to the Imperial War Museum.

He said he had been called by some people who had worked in the units but there was still a great deal of secrecy surrounding their work and few people were willing to talk about it.

The Ministry of Defence has now agreed to award defence medals to auxiliary units.

Mr Ingrams said: "It is a symbol of how secretive it was that up until now people have not been able to get any medals for it."

TOP RIGHT: *(Ref:4280/6a)* David Ingram stands by the entrance to the outdoor toilet. TOP LEFT: *(Ref:4280/3)* going down to the underground bunker. ABOVE: *(Ref:4280/1)* Mr Ingram stands inside the map room against a false wall which leads to an even more secret area used for radio communication during the war.

Courtesy ARCHANT

Axminster & Seaton News 7th March 1997
Plate 33

4
Construction

GENERAL DESCRIPTION

Investigations have revealed that the dugout was modified at some stage after initial construction, which as far as can be determined, was in 1941 at the instigation of Douglas Ingrams. Whether or not it was designed or modified by him is difficult to ascertain and although he was clearly a practical man, it is not known if he possessed any constructional, design or building expertise. Certainly the design of the dugout bears some points of similarity to a prototype which was produced by the Royal Engineers dated 28th. November, 1941.

David Ingrams, son of Douglas Ingrams, as an eleven year old schoolboy was an eyewitness and recalls that during the Easter holiday 1941 a gang of 7 or 8 soldiers were working on the site, where they excavated a large hole some 10' (3 m) below ground level, immediately alongside and to the West of a back-to-back pair of privies situated to the West of the house. It was clearly essential not to attract attention, so this excavation was almost certainly carried out by hand, without the aid of mechanical appliances, as such equipment would have been far too noisy and conspicuous. An added complication was caused by the nature of the ground material which, being greensand and comparatively easy to remove compared with clay for instance, had the disadvantage of requiring extensive shuttering and shoring to prevent subsidence – especially being so close to the Privies. In order to maintain the utmost secrecy, it was essential that the workings were not easily visible, especially from reconnaissance aircraft. The excavated material would have been very noticeable due to its light colouring and in order to alleviate this problem, it is believed the greensand some 50 cu. yds (38 cu. m.) was carefully spread on the adjacent vegetable garden and covered over with top soil. However, it seems likely that in view of the large quantity involved, it must also have been spread across the western edge of the existing adjacent slope in the ground – thus extending the slope as a bank.

Once the excavation was completed, a mass concrete slab would have been laid in situ, possibly with mesh reinforcement, but almost certainly with mild steel reinforcing rods, placed underneath the walls that were to be erected. Once the concrete had set, the walls were built up in concrete blocks, of the standard hollow twin-cell variety, measuring 9" x 18" x 9" (230 x 460 x 230 mm). Although often the practice, there is no evidence that vertical reinforcement rods were threaded down through the hollow cavities in these block walls as they were probably considered unnecessary, since the lateral compression would not have been excessive at this comparatively shallow depth. Of course, the decision to make use of this particular type of concrete block is significant, as they were clearly selected to provide some degree of thermal insulation and damp resistance. The Bewley Down dugout certainly provides good evidence of this.

The E. and W. walls of the principal chamber have concrete blockwork only 2' 3" (690 mm) high above the inside floor level and above that, they are constructed in corrugated galvanised-steel sheeting, which curves across in an arch at the top, similar to the Anderson Shelters that were made available in the built-up areas for house-owners, as a means of some protection during the Blitz. The standard Anderson Shelter was constructed in 27" (690 mm) wide corrugated galvanised-steel sheeting of 3" (76 mm) pitch (ie: between corrugations), with a metal thickness of 30 swg (Standard Wire Gauge) (0·012"/0·315 mm). These sheets curved over at the top so that, when bolted together, they formed an arch. Adjacent sheets were given an overlap of one or sometimes two corrugations, and they were erected in a hole dug in the ground, of only about 3' (1 m) depth, with the excavated soil piled over on top. Frequently they merely stood upon the earth floor, with nothing other than wooden duckboarding, or sometimes no form of flooring at all, and it was relatively unusual to find one with a concrete floor. Inevitably perhaps, they were very prone to flooding. Of course these shelters were only intended as a minimal source of protection, and would have been quite unable to withstand a direct or close hit. They were cheap and quick to erect, and must have saved thousands of lives and injuries during the Blitz.

In this case at Bewley Down, the principal chamber was covered with so-called 'Elephant' corrugated steel sheeting, which is of 5" (127 mm) pitch and heavier gauge metal – being 18 swg (0·048"/1·219 mm), which could withstand the added pressure imposed by being completely beneath

Construction

the ground surface level, with some 2' (600 mm) of backfill placed on top. These corrugated sheets provided a very quick mode of construction, as they merely had to be placed side by side, with a small overlap at the sides and top, where they were bolted together. There is one slightly odd feature regarding the fixing of this particular corrugated sheeting. On the Anderson Shelter, the bottom of each sheet, on each side, was contained within a mild steel channel which would have provided a good system of 'anchorage' when the backfill was piled up on the outside. In this case, no such channel has been included and the base of the sheets is merely contained in cement mortar on top of the concrete block walls. At first sight this seems a strange omission, and it can only be concluded that the much heavier 'Elephant' sheeting did not require such a means of containment.

One of the slight disadvantages of using metal corrugated sheeting is its tendency to attract condensation. Research was carried out during World War II, in order to try and minimise this and some special anti-condensation paints were produced which may have helped to some extent. However, this was never completely overcome and to this day the problem remains. The only real solution was to provide a complete interior lining to the corrugated sheeting, using some type of insulation board, but in fact no such measures were adopted here at Bewley Down.

A sketch (Plate 34), indicates the general arrangement within the

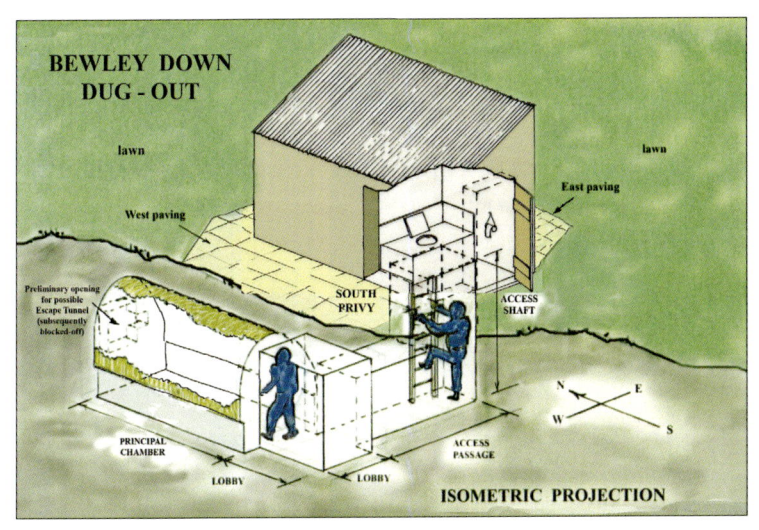

Plate 34

shelter as it was thought to have been originally constructed. It shows the vertical Access Shaft below the Privy, the short length of horizontal Access Passage leading into the Lobby with the Principal Chamber at right-angles immediately alongside. There is evidence of what was probably intended as an escape tunnel, set in the N. wall of the chamber; but it seems that the idea was abandoned as it has been rather shoddily sealed-off, merely using a flattened piece of standard 3" (76 mm) corrugated sheet which appears to have the greensand backfill placed immediately on the outside. There is no evidence of any tunnel extending away from the dugout. It should be stressed however that this illustration shows the dugout as it is thought to have been originally constructed, and differs from the layout that was subsequently created, as can now be seen. It is very difficult to give a precise date for the changes that were made, but certainly there is ample evidence of a change of use. Investigations have revealed that, at some later date, a need arose to convert the dugout so that it could accommodate a suitable wireless, which was part of the Special Duties Branch communications network. The site was codenamed CHIRNSIDE 1 and it is thought unlikely that one of the earlier forms of wireless would have been installed from the outset, but there can be no certainty about this. What has been established is that certain measures were taken in connection with the installation of a wireless, and these were after the original construction – but they could have been as a continuation of the first design. These measures are fully described in the following pages, which are of considerable interest in view of several anomalies that arise regarding the dugout, which in turn, raise a number of questions.

In considering the vertical Access Shaft, the walls of the Access Passage and Lobby are all constructed in concrete blockwork. This being so, one cannot help wondering why it was considered desirable to build the Principal Chamber using corrugated sheeting – with all the obvious disadvantages of a curved wall surface on which to fix an insulation board lining, shelving, or to display maps. Also, it seems strange that, having constructed the roof of the Access Passage and Lobby in reinforced concrete, it was thought necessary to use the 'Elephant' corrugated sheeting in the Principal Chamber. Furthermore, the 4' (1220 mm) height of the Access Passage, (just for its short length of merely 4'6" (1370 mm) seems quite pointless, when in every other part of the installation, there is sufficient

Construction

headroom. This low access can hardly have been for reasons of security, in fact all that it does achieve is a somewhat slower means of access and egress when stooping to traverse the short passage.

Continuing on the subject of roof construction over the Access Passage and Lobby, as already mentioned, this was carried out in-situ using reinforced concrete of some type (using rod or mesh). The underside of both ceilings show the clear indentation of timber shuttering that was used, on which the liquid concrete was poured, and later removed once it had sufficiently set and hardened. A layer of zinc sheeting has been found, that was laid over both the concrete and corrugated sheet roofing, which must have assisted in reducing damp penetration through the soil. Although unorthodox, this measure proved to be quite successful, as evidenced by the fact that the inside of the dugout is remarkably free from damp.

There can be little doubt that this was greatly assisted by the quite remarkable system of ventilation (Plate 35) which was included in the original design, and this is so exceptional, that it must make the dugout at Bewley Down unique, when compared with the other AU underground dugouts that have been found to survive. The ventilation system was achieved by using

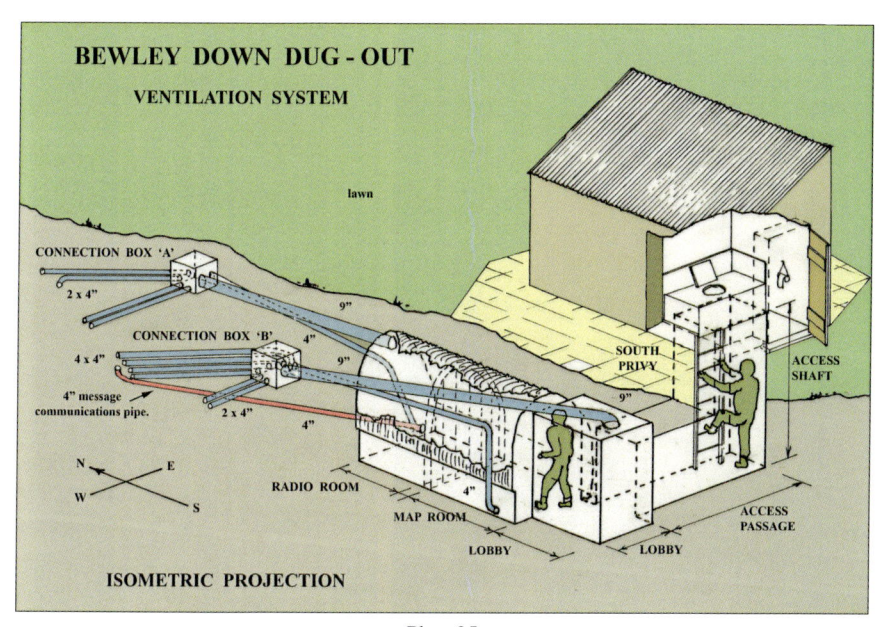

Plate 35

Connection box A
Plate 36

Connection box B
Plate 37

Construction

4" (100 mm) and 9" (230 mm) diameter piping (both glazed and unglazed), with two of the smaller pipes taken down to low level in the Principal Chamber, and with two of the larger placed at high level, thus creating an air flow by natural convection. These four pipes are then taken to a couple of small connection boxes, measuring 24" x 18" (600 x 460 mm), set a little below ground level – just to the N. of the dugout (Plates 36, 37).

From these two chambers, twin pairs of 4" (100 mm) unglazed land-drain pipes were taken over towards the edge of a W. facing bank, where they emerge, but were concealed beneath a laurel hedge, on a slight hump, which existed along the line of the bank. The hedge and hump have since been largely removed (Plate 38). It is for consideration that a greater circulation of fresh air might have been achieved if both 9" pipes were routed to one connecting box and likewise the 4" pipes to the other box.

The placing of these pipes, in order to avoid the roots, and to prevent damage (or even killing) the laurel hedge, must have been a skilled

Vent pipe terminations.
Plate 38

CHIRNSIDE 1

undertaking. Where the pipes emerge, they nearly all terminate in a NW. facing direction, which at first seems a little surprising – as the prevailing wind is from the SW. but it may have been quite intentional, as the location

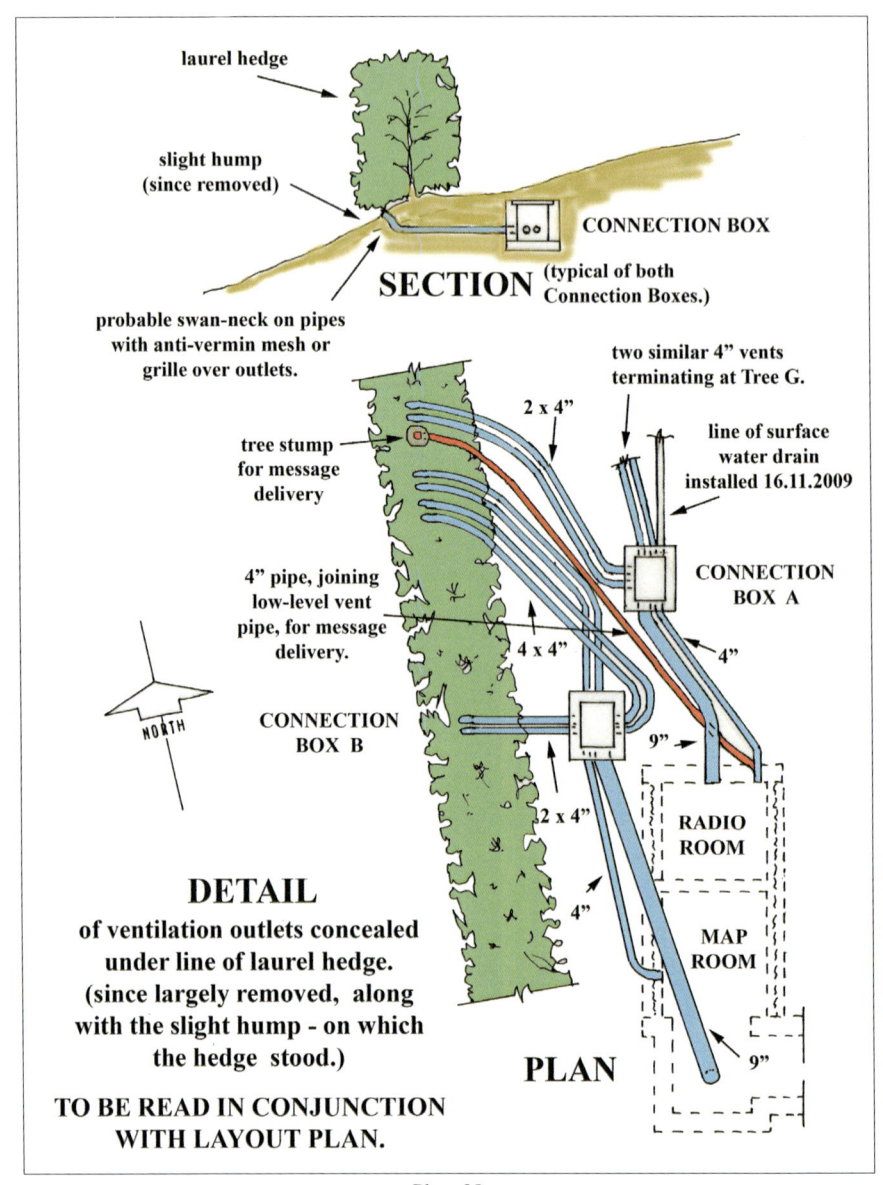

Plate 39

Construction

of SELAH is some 700 ft. (213 m.) above Sea Level and somewhat exposed. The NW orientation would therefore have avoided having too much airflow, which could have substantially lowered the temperature inside the dugout during winter months. The outlet pipes probably terminated in upstanding swan-necks, and although no traces remain, it seems likely that some form of mesh or grille would have been fitted to the outside ends of these, to prevent rats or other vermin entering the installation, which would have been particularly likely with the farm buildings in such close proximity. A preliminary survey of this ventilation system was carried out in July 2008, when the full extent of this system was revealed (Plate 39).

From the remains of some wiring found inside the dugout, it would seem that a basic form of electric lighting was available at some time, presumably with a cable, brought from the supply which would have been available in the house. No mains supply was available at that time, so a generator must have been employed, and of course this would not have raised any suspicion, as it was a common form of power supply for remote properties in the countryside. Whereas, a generator within the bunker would have raised serious problems due to its unmistakable noise and smell. Such an appliance would also have raised serious difficulties due to a build-up of CO (Carbon Monoxide) in the confined space of the dugout, despite the excellent system of ventilation. The question of heating during winter months raises a number of questions that are not easy to answer. It is stated that the dugout was lit by Tilly lamp. If this was the case significant side effects would arise as any form of Tilly lamp, paraffin heater or stove, would give off a most distinctive smell which would have been easily detectable from outside the dugout, especially at the ventilation pipes in the bank. Furthermore, these appliances generate a substantial amount of CO and water vapour, which would have been troublesome within the dugout. It can only be concluded, therefore, that additional layers of clothing were the likely means of keeping warm.

It seems probable that some form of drain would have been included to cope with flooding in an emergency, which could easily have been laid at the time of the original excavation. However, this is all supposition as no drain can be seen inside the dugout, nor any form of outlet in the lower area, which is now covered with shrubs.

CONCEALMENT

One of the most astonishing features about the dugout, which makes it unique, is the method of disguise that was adopted in order to conceal its very existence. In fact the entrance to the dugout was hidden underneath one of a pair of stone-built back-to-back Privies, which were located just a few yards due W. of the house. As already mentioned, the house was originally a pair of semi-detached cottages, and each of these had its own Privy.

On opening the outside door of the southernmost Privy, one would have been confronted with a perfectly normal wooden seat box, which extended across the opposite (N.) wall. Like most outside Privies, the inside wall surfaces were smooth flush-pointed and decorated with white lime wash, which was reasonably hygienic and easily maintained.

The extraordinary feature of this seat box, is that it could be raised vertically by some 27" (685 mm), revealing the open top void of the vertical Access Shaft. The lifting of the seat-box is achieved using a system of counter-balance weights, involving an elaborate arrangement of 0·15" (4 mm) Bowden cables and sash pulleys.

The arrangement of counterweights is positioned against the S. wall of the Access Shaft, in order not to foul or restrict the means of access, using the vertical ladder fixed on the opposite N. wall of the shaft.

RESTORATION

It is inevitable that over the course of the past seventy years, much of the original timber construction has rotted, and therefore it has been necessary to carry-out a programme of restoration in order to replicate the WWII design, construction and fittings as closely as possible. First however, it was considered desirable to undertake a complete Measured Survey of the whole installation, from which a set of drawings has been prepared (ANNEX A-3 to A-11).

In the normal process of this survey, it was necessary to very closely inspect every part of the dugout, and resulting from this, certain conclusions began to emerge. Some parts of the counterbalance system had survived, including lengths of Bowden cable and sash pulleys, although they were very rusted and corroded. Nevertheless, they provided valuable indication of sizes, lengths and positions of various components which proved

Construction

invaluable during restoration. Nothing had survived of the original seat-box in the S. Privy (Plate 40). The seat has been completely re-built, based upon the pictures and records which exist of old rural privies.

This had the usual hinged seat flap in the centre of the top, revealing the circular opening with a bucket directly beneath, and there was a hinged door in the front of the seat box, for its removal for emptying (Plate 41).

Seat-box remains – 2008
Plate 40

Restored seat-box
Plate 41

Across the back, and at each end of the seat box, there was wooden back panelling about 12" (300 mm) high, fixed to the stone walling. It has been suggested that this was a 'two-seater' Privy, but this has been discounted on the grounds that there simply would have been insufficient space.

The seat-box was supported on a light wooden frame, since replaced by metal 1½" (39 mm) Dexion angle, which is bolted to the top of four 1¼"

Dexion frame
Plate 42

Bowden cable and pulleys
Plate 43

Construction

(32 mm) diameter mild steel tubes, each with small right-angled brackets welded at their top to support the Dexion frame (Plate 42).

Using a system of counterweights, suspended on 0·15" (4 mm) Bowden cables, operating through an ingenious arrangement of sash pulleys (Plate 43). These tubes were designed to rise vertically by some 27" (685 mm), carrying the entire seat-box assembly (Plates 44, 45).

Seat-box reconstruction
Plate 44

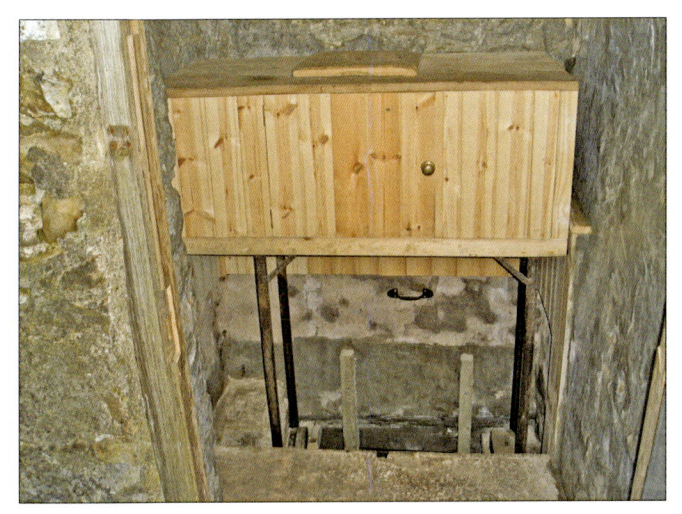

Raised seat-box
Plate 45

43

Rusting sash pulleys
Plate 46

Unrestored hoist
Plate 47

Virtually all of the Bowden cables had rusted (Plates 46, 47) and have had to be renewed but the tubes and several of the sash pulleys have been restored and put to their original use (Plate 48 – Fig. 1, 2).

Construction

RESTORED HOIST

Plate 48 – Fig. 1

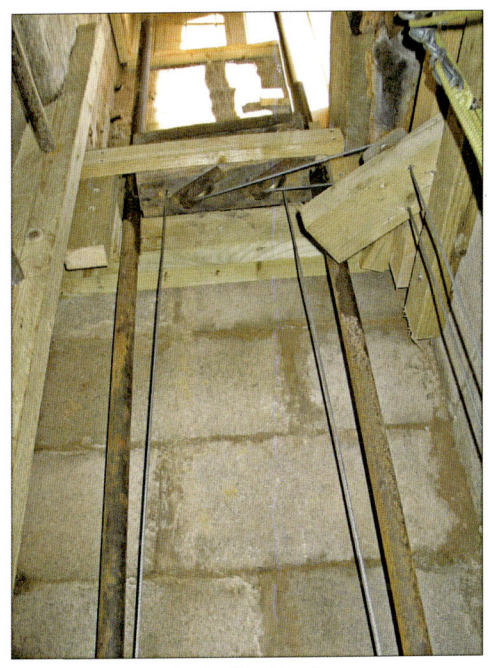

Plate 48 – Fig. 2

The counterweights used are cast lead ingots (Plates 49, 50), one of which is clearly stamped with the name of the Broken Hill Foundry in Australia (Plate 51 – Fig. 1, 2). It seems astonishing that this should have found its way to an underground dugout in East Devon.

Obsolete counterweights
Plate 49

Working counterweights
Plate 50

Construction

LEAD INGOTS

Plate 51 – Fig. 1

Plate 51 – Fig. 2

Another concealment feature concerns the fixing of the actual Privy seat-box, although it may seem highly unlikely, anyone trying to lift the box would have found, (as might reasonably be expected) that it was securely fixed in situ. In fact, raising the box to gain access to the dugout, can only be achieved by operating a long latch, which consists of a rod contained within a steel tube embedded within the concrete floor of the Privy. This rod extending some 10' (3 m) away from the outside door, terminating at the base of a concrete Rose Arbour post in a small box embedded in the ground (box added 2008) (Plates 52, 53 – Fig. 1, 2). Anyone wishing to enter the dugout, merely had to twist the curled end of the latch-rod through 90°, which turns a catch on the inside end of the rod, that engages on the frame beneath the seat-box thus securing it firmly to the ground. This catch can just as easily be operated from inside the bunker, ensuring security from possible intruders (Plate 53 – Fig. 3).

Plate 52

Construction

RELEASE ROD

Unearthed
Plate 53 – Fig. 1

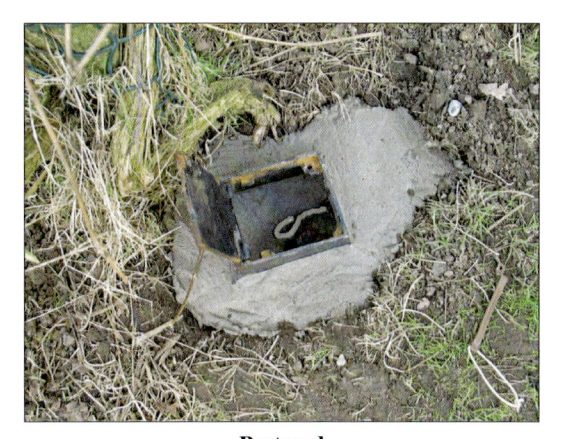

Restored
Plate 53 – Fig. 2

Catch to engage base of seat-box
Plate 53 – Fig. 3

Between the Access Passage and the Lobby was evidence of a former doorway, only part of the framing survived and that was badly affected by rot. A new frame and door have been installed, matching the original as closely as possible (Plate 54). The original latch fittings have been re-used. The purpose of this door is a matter of conjecture, it is difficult to believe that it was for 'blast proof' purposes, or that it provided a security function as a primary use. For both of these roles the construction of the door would have needed to be substantially more robust to be in any way effective. The fitting of the spring catch with a wire cable release has no obvious advantage over for instance, a simple Norfolk pattern thumb latch. The need for a barrel bolt on the inside is of questionable value, although it could have been used to stall the entry of a 'friend'. However, the door would have had some influence over noise levels, smells and airflow.

Restored Lobby door
Plate 54

LATER CONSTRUCTION

As already mentioned, the dugout was put to a different use some time after its initial build, and the measures that were taken to effect these changes were quite substantial. The main alteration was to split the Principal Chamber in two in order to provide a Map Room and Radio Room. Between them, a partition was erected consisting of old railway sleepers, with six of them arranged vertically side by side. Where these meet the underside of the corrugated ceiling, a 3" x ½" (76 x 12 mm) curved mild steel angle was fitted, to provide an 'arch'. This was only required for the purpose of retaining the upper ends of the sleepers as it certainly had no structural need whatsoever in supporting the roof. The curved sections of the angle that was used probably came from some other source, as they do not quite coincide with the curvature of the corrugated sheeting. To obviate this, a 'V' shaped notch has been cut from one section of the 'arch' so that it would fit more readily in place (Plate 55).

'V' shaped notch in angle arch
Plate 55

The Sleeper wall
Plate 56

The partition wall, composed of railway sleepers, at first glance gives the impression of being the end (N.) wall of the dugout. It is only on reflection that the trained eye might wonder why it was built in timber when all the other walls were constructed in concrete blockwork (Plate 56).

The partition wall has a small let-down table fitted to it on the Map Room side, and the original fitting has survived and operates exactly as first intended. The central two sleepers are attached together, and it is to these that the table is fixed. These two sleepers pivot at about 4'6" (1370 mm) above floor level, so that this pivotal 'door' can be partially raised, on the Map Room side, in order to allow access, although somewhat ungainly, into the Radio Room beyond (Plate 57).

Construction

Opening the Sleeper wall, to gain access to the Radio Room
Plate 57

In order to be able raise this pivotal 'door' the small table has to be let-down, otherwise it would hit the ceiling – which explains why it was made demountable. Alongside the table, on the W. wall of the Map Room there is an original let-down bench, just about long enough for someone to relax on, and it is remarkable that both this, and the table, have survived after so many years, when other timber has succumbed to wood-rot.

Special mention must be made of the method of securing this pivotal door in the sleeper wall. It is most ingenious, if somewhat 'Heath Robinson', as a drop-latch is fitted on the adjacent, fixed, sleeper on the W. side, which acts as a 'frame' for the doorway (Plate 58 – Fig. 1, 2). This drop latch is operated by a couple of pull-handles, on two quite separate lengths of 0·15" (4 mm) Bowden cable (Plate 59 – Fig. 1, 2). Quite extraordinary measures were employed to conceal the first of these, which was taken through, underneath the partition, and across the floor of the Map Room and Lobby. This cable was contained within a ¾" (19 mm) diameter steel pipe, hidden beneath a completely new floor covering, largely made up of standard 2'0" x 2'0" x 2" (600 x 600 x 50 mm) concrete paving slabs, laid upon a 1½" (38 mm) bed of sand, which in turn is laid upon a bituminous sheet of damp-proofing, placed upon the original concrete floor slab (ANNEX A-7). The cable's release mechanism was disguised in a shelf placed at about 5'0" (1520 mm) above floor level, on the S. wall of the Lobby, cleverly concealed as one of three cup-hooks set in the edge of the shelf (Plate 60 – Fig. 1. 2, Plate 61 – Fig. 1-3). The right hand hook is attached to the end of the cable, taken down below floor level, and right across under the paving slabs, to connect with the drop latch inside the Radio Room, allowing the pivotal door to be raised and opened.

CHIRNSIDE 1
RESTORATION OF SLEEPER LATCH

Plate 58 – Fig. 1

Plate 58 – Fig. 2

Construction

SLEEPER RELEASE SYSTEM

Secondary release cables
Plate 59 – Fig. 1

Primary release cables
Plate 59 – Fig. 2

RESTORATION OF SLEEPER RELEASE

Plate 60 – Fig. 1

Plate 60 – Fig. 2

CUP HOOK CABLE RELEASE

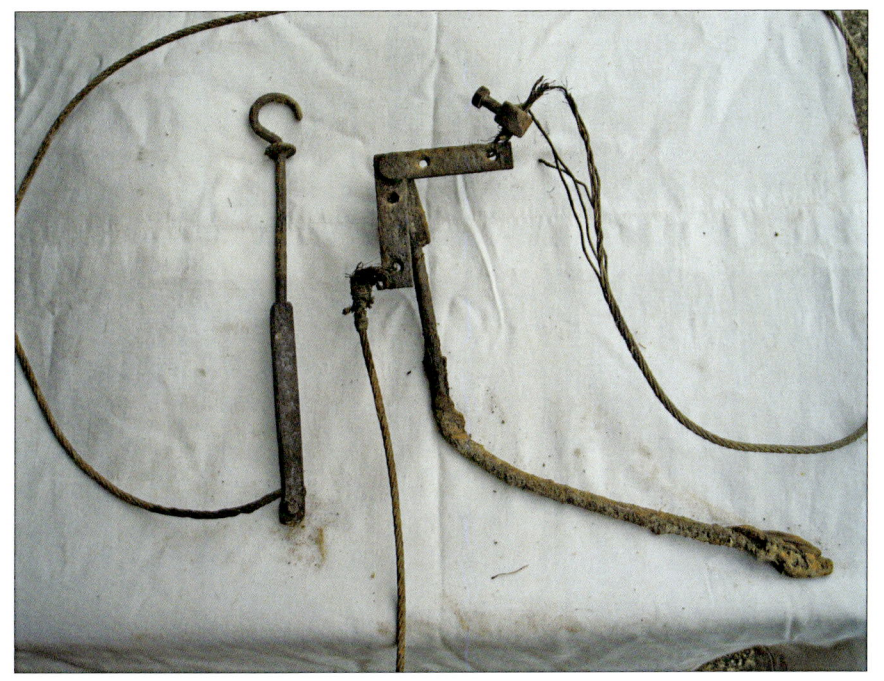

Plate 61 – Fig. 1

Plate 61 – Fig. 2

Plate 61 – Fig. 3

In effect, the whole floor level inside the Map Room, Lobby and Access Passage was raised above the original concrete floor slab by some 3½" (90 mm), just to achieve what was considered necessary concealment for this cable. However, with the advantage of hindsight, one might have thought that such measures were excessive, when for instance, a thin blade – like a hacksaw – inserted between the sleepers could have very easily raised the drop latch, to gain access. Be that as it may, it has been restored to exactly replicate the system first contrived, using several of its original components.

The floor of the Radio Room has been laid with paving slabs, in a similar manner, but separated from the Map Room by a timber threshold (rotted but restored). However, these slabs were laid on a thinner bed of sand, only about 1" (25 mm) thick, so that the floor is slightly lower than that of the Map Room. Of course there was no necessity to conceal the second cable release for the drop latch on the pivotal 'door' in the sleeper wall, and the cable was allowed to pass over the floor, at the foot of the W. wall, where it was fed into a steel pipe in the N.W. corner (Plate 62 – Fig. 1), which extends up to ground level outside the bunker (Plate 62 – Fig. 2), providing a second means of release, should the need arise, for raising the latch on the Radio Room door (ANNEX A-10).

The placing of this steel pipe, outside the N. wall of the bunker, without extensive excavation, must have been achieved by driving the tube down through the Green Sand, which would have been comparatively simple, as the backfill would hardly have become consolidated. A hole was then cut in the concrete blockwork, just above floor level in the N.W. corner of the Radio Room, where the driven pipe emerges, and it was then brought through and (rather shoddily) cemented around. Far more important from the wireless standpoint, was the need for an aerial feeder cable to be fed down into the Radio Room, and in order to achieve this, another steel pipe was driven down, outside the N. wall of the Radio Room, some 31" (790 mm) immediately to the E. of the previous pipe, and this was clearly intended for the passage of such a cable for the wireless that was then installed. Examination reveals that a half concrete block was removed from the E. side of the 'Escape Tunnel' recess revealing the edge of the flattened corrugated sheet which was used to seal off the tunnel (Plate 63 – Fig. 1) This has been roughly cut, using tin-snips or chisel, in order to get straight into the Green Sand backfill, where the bottom of the steel pipe, which had been driven down, was easily located. A right-angled bend was fitted, and a short length of steel pipe taken through horizontally into the Radio Room, where it was ideally positioned for the aerial cable to be directly

Construction

SECONDARY RELEASE FOR SLEEPER WALL ACCESS

Secondary release cable for sleeper wall
Plate 62 – Fig. 1

Above ground cable pull release
Plate 62 – Fig. 2

AERIAL FEEDER ENTRY PIPE IN N. WALL OF RADIO ROOM

Abandoned escape tunnel
and aerial pipe
Plate 63 – Fig. 1

Removed half-block and cut metal sheet
for aerial pipe access
Plate 63 – Fig. 2

connected into the wireless set (Plate 63 – Fig. 2). It is of some interest to see that a length of some 5" (130 mm) was cut off the projecting end of this horizontal pipe, as it was clearly too long and projected too far into the Radio Room. The cut off portion of the pipe was left on site, where it can be easily identified, as the angle of cut precisely fits both parts of the pipe.

All of these changes clearly had no ill-effects on the original ventilation system, as the Map Room and Radio Room each has its own 4" (100 mm) low level entry pipe, and 9" (230 mm) high level extract pipe, thus ensuring a constant flow of fresh air.

COMMUNICATION

It was clearly essential that some means of communication should be established between anyone inside the dugout and the outside world. It is a well known fact that a number of so called 'dead letter drops' were used so that runners could leave messages that could be picked up by someone who knew exactly were to find them. Sometimes these were very cleverly hidden in such unlikely places as removable stones in a wall, gate hinges, dead trees, etc., and it has been revealed that an elaborate system was adopted for the dugout at SELAH.

Mention has already been made of the twin pairs of ventilation pipes which emerge in the side of the bank under the laurel hedge. It has been discovered that *underneath* one of these pairs, there exists another pipe of 4" (100 mm) diameter, of the glazed variety, which connects directly into the low level 4" (100 mm) air inlet pipe in the N. wall of the Radio Room (Plate 64). It is recorded that messages were delivered into the Radio Room by way of this pipe. Apparently a tennis-ball which had been carefully slit so that a small slip of paper containing a message could be inserted, and then delivered via this pipe straight into the Radio Room from outside. The top of the pipe was concealed in a most ingenious way, because above

Unearthed communications pipe
Plate 64

Construction

COMMUNICATIONS PIPE TO RADIO ROOM

A section of bored tree stump (replacement), installed over the end of the pipe with the upper portion swivelling to provide access to the pipe

Plate 65 – Fig. 1   Plate 65 – Fig. 2

Message arrival point – Radio Room
Plate 65 – Fig. 3

ground level, it was fed through the centre of a dead tree-stump, about 18" (460 mm) high, with the upper 3" (75 mm) swivelling sideways to reveal the top of the pipe (Plate 65 – Fig. 1, 2). It would therefore have only taken a couple of seconds to drop the tennis-ball into the pipe leading to the Radio Room (Plate 65 – Fig. 3) (ANNEX A-11). The added advantage of this system was that security would not be compromised since the person that delivered the tennis ball would have no knowledge of the outlet.

There is no evidence to suggest that once below ground, visual communication with the outside world would be possible. Movement and sound however may well have been detectable through the ventilation system. The ability to monitor the dugout and its surrounds whether occupied or not would be a prudent security measure. The existence of a marine port hole in the west wall of the house, which overlooked the privy, may well have been installed for just this purpose (Plate 66 – Fig. 1-3).

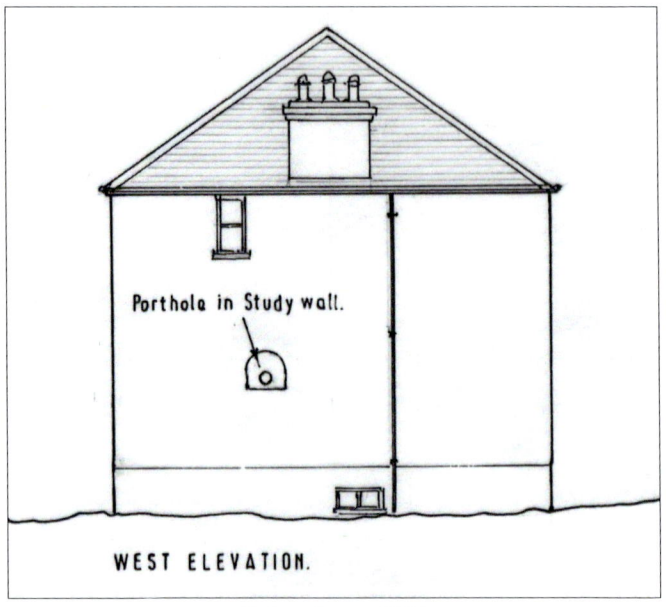

External – pre 2004
Plate 66 – Fig. 1

Internal – marine porthole
Plate 66 – Fig. 2   Plate 66 – Fig. 3

STRUCTURAL ANOMALIES

Having become so closely acquainted with the whole of the structure, during the current research, it is perhaps inevitable that certain anomalies have arisen. For instance, the actual method of construction of the vertical Access Shaft has always raised the question of exactly how this was done. Was the shaft excavated from the side of the main chamber, and 'tunnelled' upwards to break through the floor of the South Privy? Or, was it built by excavating downwards – a far more simple task. On reflection the first alternative seems fairly unlikely, as extensive shoring would have been required to prevent the walls of the Privy collapsing into the shaft. As the walls were built of random rubble stonework, they would have been particularly prone to structural damage, as there is so little bonding employed in this type of construction.

It is considered far more likely that the South Privy was probably dismantled, which would have been a relatively simple and speedy operation. The vertical Access Shaft could then be dug without fear of masonry falling into the excavation, and once the shaft was completed, the concrete replacement floor would have been laid, which as we know, contained the three metal pipes. The parts of the Privy walling that had been demolished could then be easily and quickly re-built, to blend into the remaining undisturbed part, largely comprising the North Privy. With that type of walling, it would be possible to obtain a very close match, so long as some care was taken in selecting the type and colour of sand used for the mortar, and especially the final pointing. It is significant that the whole of the random rubble stonework is pretty 'rough' and does not show great expertise on the part of the mason carrying out the work. Of course the original Privies may well have been constructed by someone, such as a fairly practical farmhand, who did not have a great deal of skill, and it is therefore interesting to realize that the re-construction of the South Privy, if indeed it was carried out as surmised, was done to carefully match the original structure, as it is built in exactly the same rather rough workmanship. Also, with regard to the quality of workmanship, the stonework of the Privies in no way compares with the skill and expertise employed in the masonry of the main house. Of course, anything other than matching stonework would have been very conspicuous, as for instance an inside lining of blockwork, which would have made the construction far easier, but obvious even to an untrained eye.

There is one further piece of evidence which tends to strengthen this suggestion. A close examination of the N. wall of the vertical Access Shaft shows that it was built 4" (100 mm) under the dividing wall between the two Privies. This would obviously have been extremely difficult if that wall had still been standing, during the construction of the Access Shaft. The reason for that 4" space is of some importance. The vertical ladder fixed to the N. wall, would have needed sufficient toe-space, beyond the actual rungs, and this could only be achieved by, either bringing the ladder further into the shaft thus reducing the available space for access, or far more likely, by simply constructing the N. wall with this 4" (100 mm) displacement, so that the shaft dimensions were not reduced, and sufficient toe-space was available for the rungs of the ladder. Again, this reinforces the suggestion that the dividing wall between the two Privies was demolished, along with the whole of the South Privy, to enable the construction to be carried out in the simplest and quickest way possible.

Another strange anomaly concerns the ventilation system. It reveals a great deal of forward planning, and considerable skill in laying the pipes through the roots of an existing Laurel hedge, with carefully concealed external upstanding swan-neck pipes, arranged to take advantage of the S.W. prevailing wind.

As described previously, the system is based upon 4" (100 mm) diameter pipes brought in at low level in the dugout's Map Room and Radio Room; with 9" (230 mm) diameter pipes placed at high level in the Lobby and Radio Room.

On the face of it, this would appear to produce a circulation of air by natural means, but the strange contradiction to this, is the fact that the two 9" (230 mm) outlet pipes terminate in Connection Box 'A' and 'B', directly alongside the 4" (100 mm) inlet pipes. This would seem to produce something of a "short-circuit", as the warm extracted air would inevitably seem to mix with the cool inlet air – thus reducing the efficiency of the whole concept of air circulation by natural convection.

There is no means of knowing if this actually occurred, and it may be that only one occupant at a time caused insufficient convection to detect any difference, because certainly the air inside the dugout is always fresh, and there is no trace of the damp smell and 'fuggy' atmosphere often associated with underground installations.

SECURITY ANOMALIES

Recorded descriptions of the dugout and its construction prior to the survey are very limited and at times conflicting. This is particularly so with regard to the latches, catches and devices which formed an integral part of the security system. The devices that have been subsequently discovered and restored, have already been fully described. Some are of obvious benefit, while others would appear to be of questionable value and perhaps even pointless. All of these are intriguing particularly when considering the thought and effort associated with their design and installation.

Entry systems: (a) Morse code entry signal.
(b) Privy seat-box release, above and below ground.

Internal systems: (c) Lobby door.
(d) Sleeper wall, below and above ground.

Morse code entry signal

The brief references to this system provide insufficient detail to allow confirmation or restoration. The description simply states:

> "...if you punch in the right code (at the foot of the rose arbour posts)... In case someone tried to gain access without punching in the right code – and the code was changed every day".

Another states:

> "...on receipt of a code (changed daily) given on a buzzer, the bell-push for which was on the pergola post near the cottage".

In addition, the following:

> "...Hidden below ground in his OB, Douglas had in view a

single battery operated bulb. Outside was a securely hidden switch – probably air-pressure actuated when pressed... a Morse code signal was arranged and changed each day".

The same author also writes:

"Those few with a need-to-know operated an actuator – David Ingrams remembered a pump like a blood-pressure bulb, hidden at ground level by the foot of a nearby rose arbour – lighting an overhead bulb in the OB, probably linked to the accumulator system. Each pressure produced a flash. A Morse code group was changed daily".

Based on what David Ingrams wrote in his lecture notes, and what he described to others, there can be little doubt that such a system existed. It is difficult however, to understand why it is described as a pneumatic device by one author, and a bell/buzzer switch by another; when there is only one known common source of information. The installation of such a signalling device would require a cable run into the Map Room. No dedicated conduit has been located and it is thought highly unlikely that the cable run would not have been hidden.

Locating the full extent of the rose arbour and position of the Morse code activator has not proved possible, however two indicators do exist. First, a concrete post supporting a metal half hoop located adjacent to the S. Privy door. Second, a buried electrical cable running from the foot of the concrete post along the southern edge of the Privy building and its adjacent small terrace on the West. It is thought that the concrete post was part of the rose arbour, and that the electrical cable was routed into the cover of the former bank and laurel hedge where access into the Map Room at floor level would easily have been gained via the 4" (100 mm) inlet ventilation pipe. Alternatively, it is possible that this cable was part of an electrical supply from the house used for a lighting circuit.

Privy seat-box release – Above ground

One publication describes:

"... twist the right coat hanger inside the privy, you can then raise the seat, bucket and contents 4ft. up in the air".

This description of the seat-box release mechanism is one of several, and once again believed to be from a common source. The release is also described as:

> "...one of the coat-hooks on the wall of the privy was hinged, and when pulled down, would activate the counterweights and raise the earth closet" (sic).

It is further described:

> "...Enter through the wooden doorway about five feet high to face the 'thunder box' and find to the left three or four hooks for coats, one of which can be pulled out an inch or so and turned to release – through a system of sturdy wires on the Bowden cable principle – a catch on the underside of the 'thunder box' allowing levers and counterbalances to operate and Hey Presto! – up moves the whole toilet arrangement to a height of about four feet".

Another description states:

> "...Inside to the left, were three cup-hooks used as coat – hangers. One was false and could be pulled and turned – if you knew about it – to operate a Bowden cable buried in the flint and concrete wall, releasing a catch".

And again by the same author:

> "...The secret approach from ground level started with a turn and tug on a wall mounted cup hook inside the door. This released a catch under the twin toilet seats".

The various details describing this release system are inconsistent and have caused speculation whilst assessing what was actually in place. Were coat hangers, coat hooks or cup hooks used? How many hooks were in place, *"three or four"* would seem to be excessive and unnecessary for a privy designed for one person? Where was the release cable run? Was a catch released, or did the cable connect directly with the hoist?

With these and other questions unanswered, close examination of the described layout revealed no evidence of such a system. The S. wall inside the privy door, is only 14" (360 mm) wide, and would be very confined for three hooks. No remnants of a cable run exist, unlike the other pulley and cable systems that have partially survived. Nor is there any indication of any attachment to the wall. The concept of coat hooks and cable as a release catch is considered somewhat unnecessary when a simple catch concealed inside the seat-box would have been more simple and equally effective. The question of how desirable it is to facilitate uncontrolled entry from above should be considered, however entry combined with the appropriate Morse code signal may have been considered sufficient security. An element of doubt over the installation of this system must remain.

There is yet another anomaly. The fact that the entire seat-box can be raised, in order to gain access down the vertical shaft, is correctly described, however the height achieved of some 4' (1200 mm) is quite impossible. The amount of vertical 'travel' is governed by the lengths of the steel tubular posts on which the seat-box is supported, and in fact, the maximum height that is possible is no more than 27" (690 mm). One cannot help wondering where did this figure of 4' originate?

Quite unexpectedly during restoration of the site, a closer examination of the privy floor revealed yet another hidden release mechanism, of which there is no known description. Set in the concrete floor of the S. Privy, there are three metal pipes laid horizontally in a N-S direction, and the ends of these can be clearly seen in the edge of the floor, at the top of the Access Shaft (Plate 67). In fact, these had been assumed to be a form of reinforcement for the concrete floor slab.

However, investigation has revealed that the most westerly pipe, of ½" (12 mm) diameter, has a metal rod inside it, and this had plainly been cut off flush with the S. wall face of the vertical Access Shaft. This pipe (and its inside rod) extends for some 10' (3 m) from the Privy doorway, and terminates at the base of a concrete arbour post, the internal rod ending in a bent loop, so that it can be twisted through 90° to release a catch under the seat-box. This system has been completely restored.

The other two pipes which are of ¾" (20 mm) diameter, are of differing lengths, the easterly one extending for 18" (460 mm) and the central one for 36" (920 mm) beyond the Privy door threshold. The purpose of these two pipes has not yet been determined, but the discovery of the long control rod,

Metal pipes in privy floor
Plate 67

operating the catch under the seat-box certainly brings into question the need for a second 'coat hook' system. The possibility of confusion after the passage of time cannot be discounted, and perhaps the 'above ground coat-hook system' never existed, and has been confused with the below ground cup-hook sleeper wall door release. Investigations show that the hitherto undescribed/undiscovered pipe and rod was the sole release system.

Privy seat-box release – below ground

The ability to operate the seat-box hoist from below, to allow entry has been stated, and this was an obvious and necessary facility. The reconstructed hoist system allows simple operation both to raise and lower. An individual standing underneath the seat-box has the counterweights conveniently situated, allowing for them to be pushed up or pulled down, thus operating the hoist. Reference is made to a catch system that was operated by the individual descending the Access Shaft.

"....On his way down, the operator encouraged the counter-weight to ease the toilet-seats, complete with bucket-and-chuck-it, back into position, and then secured the catch".

Other than having access to a catch fitted for use by an 'incoming' person, there is no evidence of there ever having been a dedicated catch system for operation from below.

Lobby door

Once access via the ladder in the vertical Access Shaft has been achieved, entry into the Map Room is through a wooden door serving the Lobby.

"…go along a short passage, pull taut an overhead wire which sprang open a door and let you into a map room with supplies, books and a bed".

No other reference nor description of this door is known. Prior to reconstruction, all that had survived was the door frame, still attached to the walls, and a broken length of wire rope threaded through the frame, through a small metal tube, with a brass spring catch fitted to one end. Both a spring catch keep and a bolt keep have survived. A replacement door has been constructed from salvaged elm floor-boards, and a new frame fitted with both spring-catch and bolt. The release wire has been replaced with matching Bowden cable, and threaded through the door frame, re-using the same small metal tube. The only change made is for this cable to be run in a horizontal line (rather than overhead) for convenience.

Sleeper wall – below ground

The release system for the door in the sleeper wall is without doubt intriguing. An ingeniously concealed system of wires and levers result in a working system, but once again the same result could have been achieved in a far more simple way without the intricate installation. The task of restoring this system has been hindered by a lack of information. Surprisingly, it appears not to have attracted the attention of those who have provided the descriptions of other catches and latches. Some of the scant details are incorrect and other obvious detail has not been described, which poses a number of questions. Attempts have been made to answer these, together with plausible explanations. In his lecture notes, David Ingrams surprisingly omits any description of entry into the Radio Room, and likewise Derrick Warren makes no mention of the latch system. In fact, it is only John Warwicker who states :

> "...At the entrance of the map room is a shelf with three brackets. One is ingeniously false and rotates – releasing more counterweights and permitting the two end railway sleepers to grind open, revealing a narrow entrance into the restricted space of the radio room".

He later writes two other descriptions of the system, but in different terms:

> "...However, a small lever was hidden underneath the table. When pulled, it released the catch securing a secret access cover, allowing a second system of weights and counter balances to activate. These lifted a disguised hatch, and permitted access to a small, one-person space of the radio room". "...to the main chamber where another hidden catch could be activated to bring further counterweights into play. With these, a section of the railway-sleeper far wall rolled away on a monorail to reveal a small radio room".

In considering the various descriptions, and with the benefit of having conducted a detailed survey of the site and materials, it is suggested that the many and varied inconsistencies are probably due to the passage of time. There are, in addition, statements and descriptions which require closer scrutiny.

No evidence of a lever hidden beneath the table in the Map Room has been found, and it is thought doubtful that a third release system for the Radio Room latch would have been necessary. The access into this room through the sleeper wall has been described as being operated with the use of weights, counter balances and a monorail. Once again, no evidence of these has been found, and in any case the use of weights and counter balances would have been particularly difficult to install in such a confined space, and unless of unrealistic proportions, would not have provided any particular advantage. The two sleepers which are movable, are simply pivoted at about three-quarters of their overall height, so that they can be raised and lowered by one person with relative ease, on the Map Room side, but admittedly less so from the Radio Room.

Sleeper wall – above ground

During the survey, a secondary catch release system for the sleeper wall door was found, which has not been previously recorded nor described. It is believed that the importance of having a release operated from above ground was rightly realised and thus installed. Consisting again of a wire cable and pulley, the wire entered the Radio Room from above, through a 1" (25 mm) diameter metal pipe behind the N. wall of the Radio Room which was linked to the common latch. In the event of the below ground release system being damaged/broken, the latch to the Radio Room door could be released by pulling the wire from above ground.

COSTING CONSIDERATIONS

We know from David Ingram's recollections that when he came home from boarding school, for his Easter holiday, a gang of seven or eight soldiers were digging an enormous hole beside the old original Privy. Speedy working would have been essential and as the work was carried out in Springtime there was the advantage of extra daylight hours due to the introduction of Double British Summertime. Also, of course, there was a paramount need for complete secrecy, which prevented the use of large mechanical equipment, although clearly this would have greatly assisted in speeding-up the constructional process. It is likely that the soldiers were Sappers of the Royal Engineers, as there was really no other branch of the army that could provide a workforce with the necessary skills. Also, this would have prevented any civilian or outside tradesmen from being employed, and would have minimised the risk of "careless talk" and loss of security. The excavation has been calculated at a bulk measurement of some 50 cubic metres, consisting mainly of Greensand, some of which would have been retained and used as backfill. The remainder and by far most of that bulk amount would have had to be spread, and the very conspicuous excavated material, would have had to be concealed from aerial observation by immediately covering it with topsoil. Achieving this would have entailed

Construction

many additional hours of work, when compared with 'normal' excavation projects.

The following constructional tasks would have had to be accomplished:
1. Excavation, disposal, and concealment of material.
2. Concrete base laid – site mix, and reinforcement.
3. Hollow concrete blockwork erected.
4. Erection of corrugated steel sheeting to principal chamber.
5. Installation of ventilation system – a considerable task in itself.
6. Backfill with support against tunnel entry.
7. Demolish S. Privy, and set aside material for subsequent re-use.
8. Excavate for entrance shaft, removing material.
9. Build shaft and access passage, with concrete shuttering for roof of latter.
10. Lay concrete S. Privy floor, and re-build walls to match former structure, blending the re-constructed work into the existing N. Privy stonework.
11. Complete all internal fittings and components.
12. Final installation of necessary equipment.

Using current production allowances per hour of various labours and costed at £15·00 together with an assessed cost of materials, it is suggested that the overall cost, without mechanical assistance, would have been in the order of £45,000·00, although at a current charging out rate, labour would have been nearer £20·00, if indeed, manual labour could be found to undertake such work. It should be remembered however, that modern Health & Safety regulations would have demanded the provision of far more stringent precautions in shoring the excavations, and a completely different attitude to the general welfare than would have been likely in wartime conditions.

5
Wireless and Electrical Installation

BACKGROUND

The first wireless to be used at Bewley Down was the TRD transceiver which was probably installed in the summer of 1942. With the arrival of the TRD, the site initially operated as an OUT-Station (CHIRNSIDE 1) of the CHIRNSIDE network which had its CONTROL or IN-Station (CHIRNSIDE 0) at Castle Neroche, some 7 miles (11·3 Km) to the North. The TRD was a battery operated set used for voice communication, operating between 48 and 65 MHz; the use of this frequency band limited communication to near line of sight between transmitter and receiver aerials. Its distinguishing characteristic was an unusual form of modulation that gave a measure of speech security. The TRD used rechargeable 6v 75AH secondary batteries (accumulators) that could be used continuously for some 12 hours on a full charge. Each station had 3 batteries giving a maximum operating time of about 36 hours. No onsite charging facilities were provided.

Later on in 1943, it is thought that a type WS17 wireless was also installed at Bewley Down. With this additional equipment, CHIRNSIDE 1 then became an intermediate or RELAY Station to the new SUB-OUT-Station CHIRNSIDE 1A at Axminster 4·5 miles (7·2 Km) to the South. The WS 17 set is a battery operated voice transceiver using a similar frequency band of 44-61 MHz, and thus also needed a near clear line of sight between the aerials of the two sets. The WS 17 was designed for use between searchlight section HQs and detachments and had a nominal range of about 3-5 miles depending on the aerial used. The set used ordinary amplitude modulation so was not able to communicate directly with the TRD. The batteries used were a 120 volt dry battery and a 2 volt 75AH accumulator. The dry battery gave some 300 hrs of operation and the accumulator 150 hrs (2 were provided).

Both sets were simplex transmitter/receiver (not possible simultaneously) and were designed for simple operation by users with a minimum of training. Specifications of the WS17 are well known since several working original sets exist (Plate 68), however, details of the TRD are not known as all records and sets were dumped and sealed in a coalmine by Capt. Ken Ward. The research that continues into producing an exact replica is dependant on scarce personal memories (Plate 69).

WS17
Plate 68

TRD Replica
Plate 69

Investigation into the construction of the dugout strongly suggests that its division into two sections separated by a sleeper wall was a subsequent alteration. There is no evidence as to when this was done, but it is assumed that it coincided with the first TRD wireless installation.

Radio Room electrical fittings
Plate 70

Map room electrical fittings
Plate 71

ELECTRICAL CABLES AND FITTINGS

No direct electrical evidence of the wireless installation below ground remains. However, a quantity of loose wiring and fittings has survived but there is no indication that it was used for anything except general lighting (Plates 70, 71).

The fittings do not suggest any particular operating voltage. The house was not connected to 240v 50Hz mains until well after the war, so it is likely that this lighting installation would have used a battery DC supply to avoid a generator having to be run whenever the dugout was occupied, most probably as an extension of whatever electric lighting was used in the house. The house system and farm buildings are likely to have used large 24v accumulators for night-time operation, charged during the day with a motor generator set, a common arrangement for businesses needing lighting in rural areas at that time. This theory is supported by a section of moderately heavy duty 2 core rubber insulated cable that was found buried

Uncovered 2 core rubber insulated cable
Plate 72

2 core rubber insulated cable
Plate 73

alongside the south privy entrance (Plates 72, 73), this may have been the supply to the dugout.

A local report suggests that a field telephone link may have existed between the dugout and the house. The 2 core cable could have been used for this link but its size would be unnecessarily large for a telephone. There is no other evidence of a telephone link.

Nothing has been found to suggest permanent or professionally installed wiring within the dugout. However there may have been a temporary or portable system which could be deployed when circumstances allowed. Such a system is supported by the position of one of the surviving cables which had been threaded between the Lobby door frame and the wall in what appears to be an 'informal' route (Plate 74). This cable might have been the supply or for a light switch at the entrance shaft.

There is no remaining evidence of a specific conduit for the cable to enter the dugout, although one of two steel tubes set in the concrete floor of the south privy threshold could have afforded entry.

Lobby wiring behind door frame
Plate 74

The cable discovered buried adjacent to the south privy door, is unprotected and at a shallow depth suggesting it was a later addition and may have entered the dugout through one of the ventilation pipes concealed in the base of the hedge. Further evidence may well have been lost when the hedge was removed (circa 2002). This cable might have been part of the entrance signal bell or buzzer system that was known to exist.

Whilst there is clear evidence that electrical power was provided to the dugout there is no evidence to suggest that it was an operational necessity. On the contrary, wirelesses were battery powered and the use of Tilley lamps for lighting is described as the norm for this and other sites.

The electric lighting was possibly installed when longer periods of manning were needed for the operation of the wirelesses. This is likely to have coincided with the installation of the WS17 and the extra link to

CHIRNSIDE 1A. However the evidence on manning is ambiguous. It may be that prearranged time schedules were used for wireless watches at all OUT-Stations but this would have been unsatisfactory in times of higher alert status owing to the potential delay in forwarding messages whilst awaiting the next schedule. There is firm evidence from the house visitors book that ATS wireless staff from Volis Farm, who were involved in manning the IN-Station, were visitors to Bewley Down but apparently only in a social sense, since they are on record as never having visited the wireless station. 24 hr manning was ordered in Dec 1943 but by Feb 1944, Douglas Ingrams was away in Norfolk replacing John Collings as Special Duties Branch IO. It is not known who manned CHIRNSIDE 1 in his absence although Capt E.C. Grover took over as IO in this area having been moved from Northumberland. If CHIRNSIDE 1 was put onto 24 hr manning, for which there is little firm evidence, lighting by Tilley lamps would have presented problems with fumes, and re-fuelling, so that the use of electric light would have become almost essential. In addition, the batteries powering the wireless sets would have needed changing and re-charging after a relatively short time – less than 24 hrs of continuous use for the TRD. There were insufficient batteries for this, so it is more likely that pre-arranged wireless communication schedules became more frequent, but not continuous, in times of increased tension. The IN-Stations were much better equipped with mains or generator power supplies and staff for continuous listening and they would have been able to respond to emergency messages from OUT-Stations at any time.

AERIALS

Excavations have revealed an empty vertical 1" (25 mm) iron pipe leading down from ground level to the alcove in the North wall of the Radio Room. This is thought to have been a later addition associated with the creation of the Radio Room. The probable use was as a duct for the wireless aerial feeder cable(s) (Plate 75).

It has been suggested that there were originally three trees that had aerials installed within them. All three trees are still present (ANNEX A-3). Only two trees, the North Aerial Tree 'E' and South Aerial Tree 'B' exhibit clear signs of aerial installation. Both trees are Scots Pines (Plate 76). The

Wireless and Electrical Installation

Radio room aerial feeder pipe
Plate 75

Aerial site
Plate 76

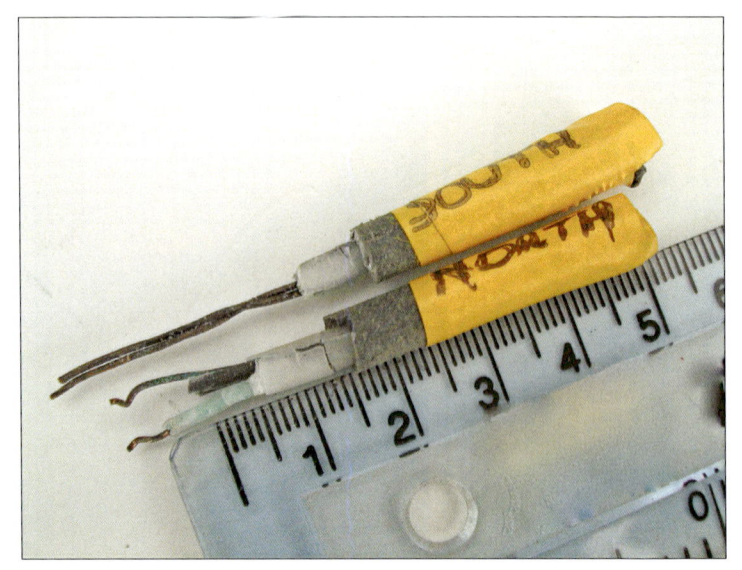

North and South tree aerial feeder specimens
Plate 77

aerial associated with the North tree appears to have been about 30ft (9.1m) above ground, while that of South tree was probably rather lower at about 20ft (6·1m).

Feeder cables

The aerial associated with the North tree was definitely connected by a circular twin conductor unscreened cable; some sections of this are still buried in the ground and lead up the tree.

The materials and construction of this cable are definitely those of a radio frequency (RF) cable such as were developed from about 1938 onwards. The two conductors are individually insulated, with different colours, and enclosed in a special plastic dielectric material (probably polyethylene) used to reduce the cable's electrical velocity factor and to minimise losses. This type of cable has low characteristic impedance (probably near 75 Ohms) so that it would present a good impedance match to the centre of a half wave dipole. Thus it would have been suitable to directly feed such an aerial from the aerial terminals of the transmitter/receiver. It serves the same purpose as the contemporary descriptions of a flat twin 80 Ohm cable (made by Belling Lee) that was said to be used with the TRD. Both of these types of feeder are said to be 'balanced' because they are symmetrical both electrically and physically. Circular twin conductor cable, like that associated with the North aerial tree at Bewley Down, has been found on many Auxiliary Unit wireless sites. It is often, but incorrectly, described as co-axial cable – the two conductors are NOT concentric and there is no overall metallic screen.

Sections of a single conductor circular cable have also been found buried leading to the base of the South aerial tree; however, although the external appearance is similar, it is actually quite different. Although it has two strands of solid copper wire, these are not insulated from each other. They form a single conductor located within an inner plastic RF dielectric material, (again probably polyethylene), together with an overall plastic protective cover like the twin conductor version (Plate 77).

If one of these single conductor cables had been installed originally as the only feeder for whatever aerial was in the South tree, then this would be an unbalanced arrangement owing to the lack of electrical symmetry: it would be most unusual to feed a VHF aerial operating in the band 50 – 70 MHz in this manner. A single wire unbalanced aerial feeder (suspended in free air) is sometime used at HF in a configuration known as a Windom aerial, but it has to be set up with care and is also dependent on a good RF ground connection at the transmitter. It is very unlikely that this approach would have been used at 50 – 70 MHz, and the burying of the single feeder wire directly in the ground (or a metal pipe) would have been severely detrimental to its performance. It is most unlikely that a single wire feeder was actually used on this site.

It is more likely that the single extant cable is one of two that were used originally to form a twin conductor pair of cables; these might have been laid alongside each other, or slightly twisted, to form a balanced feeder which would suit both the balanced (symmetrical) dipole aerial and the balanced aerial circuits of the transmitter and receiver. Such an arrangement of two cables laid side by side would have a slightly higher characteristic impedance (about 75 – 90 Ohms); this makes it more likely to have been used with the WS17 which also had medium impedance output circuits.

There is however no physical evidence that a pair of the single conductor cables was used for the South aerial. It is possible that removal of the hedge in the 2000's, through which the aerial cables would have passed, just removed one cable of this loosely laid pair from the ground.

There is some support for this theory from Yorkshire. Photographic evidence from the Sigglesthorne OUT-Station shows four circular cables protruding from the aerial feeder pipe into the bunker, but the internal detail of these cables is not recorded. At this site there are only two trees with firm evidence of aerials, hence the implication that each aerial had a feeder comprising two cables forming a balanced pair.

It is possible that the single conductor cable was developed earlier and might have been more readily obtainable than the more physically complex two conductor variant. If the South feeder and aerial were installed first, it could have been used with the TRD, and then later swapped for use with the WS17 because both sets used the same frequency band and they were communicating in reciprocal directions. However, using the South tree for communication in a northerly direction would not be a natural choice because of the other trees immediately north of the South tree that would add to the signal attenuation in a northerly direction. The presence of foliage, particularly if wet, can reduce signal strengths appreciably; furthermore nearby tree trunks (especially when wet) can also act as undesired parasitic aerial elements if vertical aerials or polarisation is used. It is far more likely that aerial trees with horizontal elements would have been chosen on the edge of the copse on the side nearest the remote station and connected to the set normally used for that link.

In the event of an aerial becoming unserviceable, it might have been possible to use the aerial normally used with the other set but the quality of communication would have been poor.

North Aerial Tree

From the base of this tree the twin conductor feeder cable (with minor breaks) was found to lead in a southerly direction for approx 11'8" (10·5m) (Plate 78). The exact route of the cable beyond this point has not been established, but it is thought likely that it passed under the laurel hedge and entered the Radio Room via the 1" (25mm) vertical pipe already described.

Wireless and Electrical Installation

Exposed feeder cable
Plate 78

NORTH TREE FEEDER CABLE

Plate 79 – Fig. 1

Plate 79 – Fig. 2

Plate 79 – Fig. 3

At the base of the tree the cable surfaces and runs vertically until about 4'6" (1·3m) off the ground where a short horizontal step is made before continuing vertically towards the nest-box (Plate 79 – Fig. 1). Just above the nest-box the cable makes another short horizontal step to bring it to the last vertical section on the north side of the trunk (Plate 79 – Fig. 2). There is no evidence in this tree of the use of staples to secure the cable in the bark layer. The reason for the lower dog-leg in the cable route is not known, but is probably some aspect of concealment associated with the hedge. The upper dog-leg might have been to increase the separation between feeder cable and the wires of the actual aerial.

When originally installed, the cable is believed to have been placed in a grove in the bark and then sealed with resin and plaster of Paris which subsequently caused an unequal growth rate of the bark and hence the clearly defined cable line and scar. The two insulated conductors of this feeder cable are clearly evident (Plate 79 – Fig. 3). No remains exist of the actual aerial elements associated with this feeder, either in this tree or in the other nearby third tree F. The aerial elements were probably made of hard drawn copper wire slung between suitable branches. The main aerial element would have been a half-wave dipole of overall length 7'9" (2.2m) with each arm connected, at its centre; one side to each wire of the aerial feeder described above.

At the ends of the aerial wires, there are likely to have been egg or insulating link insulators for attaching the supporting rope leading to suitable branches – metallic wire rope supports are unlikely to have been used to avoid extraneous parasitic aerial elements. The aerial elements were probably horizontal. The aerial elements could have been vertical but is thought most unlikely – it makes it much harder to route the feeder away perpendicular to the aerial elements in the confines of a tree, and also increases the chance of undesirable alterations of the aerial radiation pattern due the presence of tree trunks in the immediate forward direction.

Ken Ward states categorically that the aerials for the TRD were always horizontal; the reason being to make the most of the directional properties of a horizontal dipole. In idealised free space, maximum signal strength occurs uniformly in all directions perpendicular to a single dipole element; this means that a single horizontal dipole gives best signals overhead and perpendicular to it towards both horizons (ignoring ground and tree effects). The successful installation of such VHF aerials into these trees would almost certainly have followed temporary trials before final installation of the feeder cables and equipment into the dugout. There are contemporary reports of unsuccessful trials and the need for alternative aerial and equipment locations at Briscoe's Farm not far away in West Dorset.

Apart from other trees on the north side of the spinney at this site, the radio path between these aerial trees and Castle Neroche is unlike the ideal case of crossing a deep valley. The ground level along the top of the Bewley Down is close to the actual line of sight and so is unlikely to have been a good radio path with plain dipole elements at both ends, probably leading to unreliable communication. This means that an additional reflector element is likely to have been needed at CHIRNSIDE 1 to increase signal strengths in both directions – especially when the trees were wet or full of sap. The addition of a passive reflector element would improve performance significantly in the chosen direction, which depends on the relative positions of the dipole and its reflector.

The reflector would have been about 8'6" (2·6m) long and also made of copper wire, spaced about 2' to 3' (0·6 – 0·9m) from and parallel to the main dipole (Plate 80); it would have been suspended in a similar manner. The reflector element does not need to be connected to anything else; hence it would not have had its own feeder cable. The use of a reflector to enhance performance to the North, would also reduce radiation southwards towards enemy occupied France and would also attenuate unwanted signals to/from other users of those frequencies off the sides of aerials. This might have helped avoid interference to other nearby users of these frequencies. (It is unlikely that the aerials used at Castle Neroche could have had a reflector fitted because of their need for much wider coverage in azimuth to other distant stations.)

For the link to the North, any reflector element would have to be located south of the main dipole aerial connected to the feeder cable. In the video film recorded by David Ingrams in 1999, he indicates that there were three 'aerial' trees and points to both Scots pines E and F. Tree E has the feeder cable installed in it, so it is probable that the feeder led from tree E high up across to the main dipole radiating element strung between the branches of the third tree F; this would have allowed the reflector element to be hung from the branches of tree E with approximately the desired spacing of about 3'9" (1·1m) in from the main dipole.

This arrangement would have operated satisfactorily to the North and

Wireless and Electrical Installation

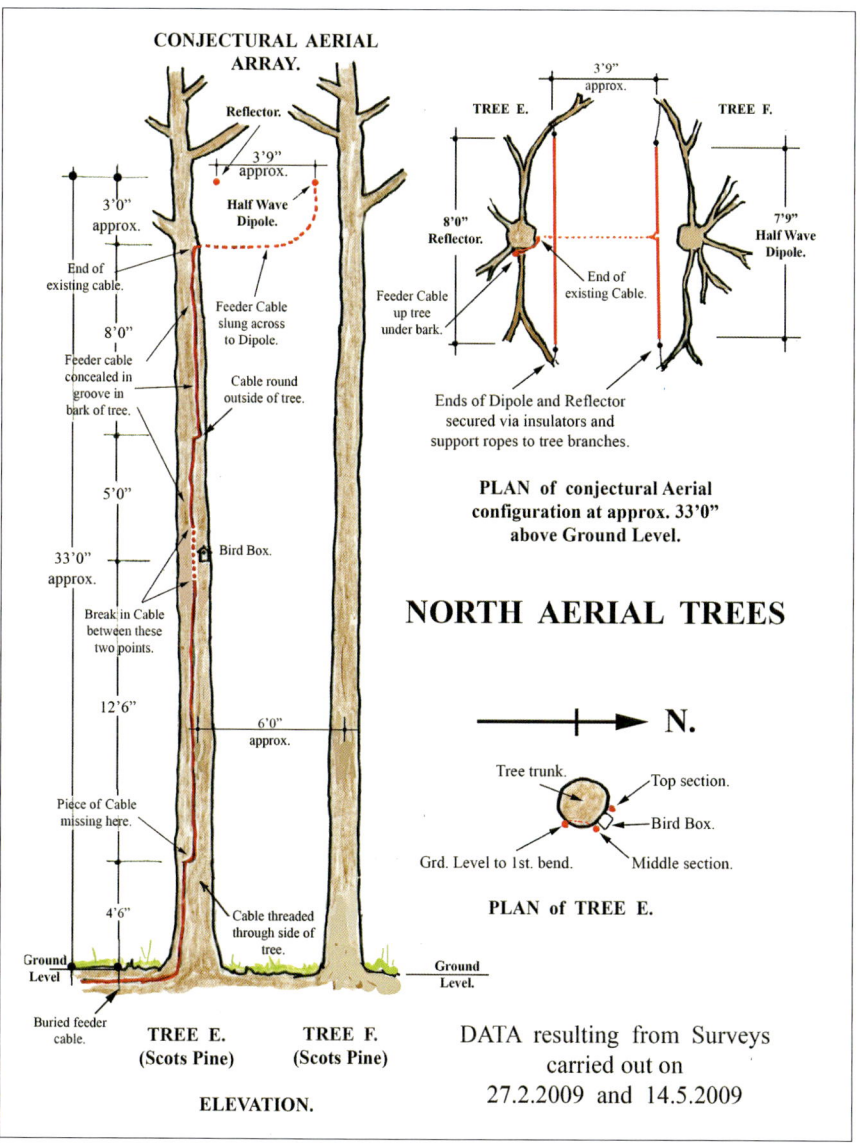

Plate 80

is consistent both with the surviving evidence and the record of there being three aerial trees. There is no surviving evidence in either tree E or F, of either the main dipole that was attached to the feeder, the passive reflector element, or any supporting arrangements.

CHIRNSIDE 1

No evidence or suggestion of standby aerials has been found at this site to cater for weather damage; since both the TRD and WS17 used the same frequency band, it is possible that the aerial of either set might have been tried with the other in an emergency.

ALTHOUGH THERE IS NO EVIDENCE, THIS TREE PROBABLY HAD A HORIZONTAL DIPOLE AERIAL, WITH E. - W. ORIENTATION, SUPPORTED BY THE BRANCHES.

TREE B.
(Scots Pine)

N.W. ELEVATION   N.W. - S.E. SECTION

SOUTH AERIAL TREE

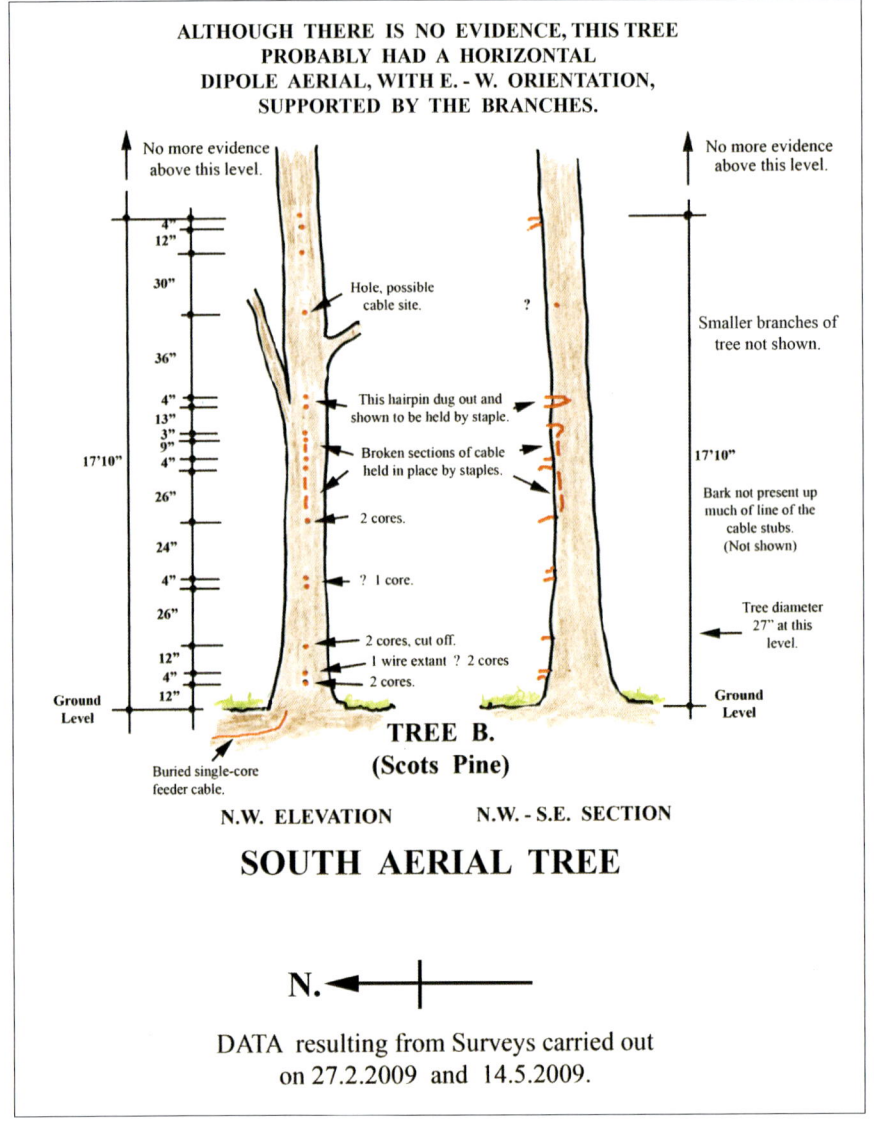

N. ←——|——

DATA resulting from Surveys carried out on 27.2.2009 and 14.5.2009.

Plate 81

South Aerial Tree

The evidence found in this tree is completely different from that of the North tree and at first sight is somewhat of an enigma (Plate 81). The feeder cable that has been found leading to this tree was buried 6" (15cm) below ground and the remains are of the single conductor variant. However, the evidence in the South aerial tree is mostly short sections of the other type of twin conductor RF type cable – there are many protruding ends of cables sticking out horizontally from the outer surface of the tree.

The change of feeder cable type, from the presumed two single conductor types laid together, over to a single twin conductor cable, would appear to have occurred near ground level. There is no surviving evidence of this junction. It is presumed that twin conductor version was used in the tree because it was easier to conceal.

For much of the tree's height in the region of these cables, the bark is missing revealing a smooth surface of the younger growth of the tree (Plate 82); this wood is partially decayed which has permitted limited excavation into the trunk to ascertain the route of the cable.

Base of South tree
Plate 82

Excavated cable loop and staple
Plate 83

In at least two instances, the pairs of extant cables are formed into a loop currently buried about 4 – 6" (10 – 15cm) deep into the trunk with a spacing of 3" (7.5cm) between the ends, rather like a large 'hairpin'. One loop is still held in place by a staple (Plate 83). It will also be noticed that the scar, where the cable was installed, is very different to that of the North aerial tree despite them being the same species of tree.

For much of its height, the bark in the region of the cable on the South tree, has died away revealing the softwood of the trunk. This may suggest the cable was installed at a different time of year – possibly when the sap was up, with the tree growing actively in the summer months, thus causing a bigger scar, or possibly less skilful concealment. Many of the loops are spaced 13" (33cm) apart (Plate 84), with the lowest just 12" (30cm) off the ground.

It is possible that some of these solitary protruding cables (those which are not obviously paired in a loop) do have the other end of a loop covered

Wireless and Electrical Installation

Cable ends in middle of South tree
Plate 84

up just below the existing tree surface formed by the youngest wood. The distance between the existing remnants corresponds roughly to a regular pattern upwards on the trunk to a height of about 18' (5·5m) – namely 13" (33cm) gaps between 3" (7·5cm) wide loops. The small amount of remaining vertical sections of the feeder cable are stapled direct to cracks in the bark; in one case it bends abruptly towards the centre of the tree at one side of a

Partially excavated loop
Plate 85

loop (Plate 85) but this maybe the result of natural tree growth. The internal constructions of all the sections of cable, which can be easily seen in this tree, are similar to the two conductor North feeder cable.

The more likely possibility is that this pattern of remains is the result of natural tree growth. Tree growth occurs in successive years on the outside just below the bark; so if the cable had been stapled at regular 13" intervals just below the bark, over the years, the staples would remain at the same distance from the centre of the tree with that section of cable between the staples being pushed outwards by the new growth. This would stretch the cable, eventually causing it to snap after many years, so allowing the cable ends (either side of a staple) to ultimately emerge many years later horizontally from the tree's surface. Securing a cable at about 10 – 13" (25 – 33cm) intervals would be typical practice by a skilled tradesman for the conventional installation of this weight/type of cable. Often the shaft of a hammer handle is used as convenient measuring tool to decide where the next staple should be placed. It is also possible that exposed sections of cable might have been intentionally cut out and removed at stand-down. This would increase the likelihood of the tree's development and pattern of cable ends as recorded here (Plates 86, 87). There are many instances

Wireless and Electrical Installation

Snipped off cable – South tree
Plate 86

Cable ends – South tree
Plate 87

elsewhere of barbed wire showing similar patterns many years after being stapled to growing trees. The aerial trees at other AU wireless sites where the feeder cables were concealed in the bark also exhibit regular patterns, but the appearance depends on the tree species. For example, those at Sigglesthorne in Yorkshire are oaks – they display a 'bump' in the bark at the probable staple locations.

If the South tree originally had some other sort of aerial assembly, it would have needed extra wires or vertical radiating elements between these loops with a very regular pattern. The loop spacing might suggest a much higher operating frequency (about 400MHz) which is unlikely in close proximity to a tree. As frequency is increased, dimensional stability and rigidity of the aerial array are increasingly important, but there is nothing to suggest that additional mountings or extra metallic features were ever present. There is no onsite or documentary evidence to support much higher frequency operation, or other radio facilities, apart from simple VHF radio links using the TRD or WS17.

Given the unlikelihood of operation at very much higher frequencies, it is reasonable to assume that the existing remains are those of a single feeder cable that was originally buried and stapled just below the bark which has been grown 'over' then cut or snapped during subsequent years.

There is nothing to suggest what aerial elements might have been connected at the top of the South aerial tree. It is more likely that this installation was provided after the initial TRD facilities, and that the South tree was used with the WS17 set to provide communication with the SUB-OUT-Station at Axminster. The main half wave dipole element for the WS17 would have had the same dimensions as that for the TRD, i.e. 7'9" (2·4 m) overall. Its construction and method of mounting would have been the same as for the North tree. The shorter and less obstructed radio path to Axminster makes it unlikely that reflectors would have been needed at either end. The surviving nearby trees do not give any indication whether the aerial was horizontal or vertical: the WS17 could be used with either, but horizontal might have given slightly better signal strengths in the desired southerly direction. It is also unclear whether this aerial was supported by the South aerial tree or by other trees that are no longer present.

When both sets were on the site, the WS17 would have used the southern aerial and the TRD the northern one with reflector. This would avoid the possibility of either radio path being masked by the other's aerial.

SUMMARY

Immediately prior to stand down in 1944, it is likely that:–

a) Electric Lighting was provided by an extension of the house's 24v DC system.

b) Communication with CHIRNSIDE 0 used the TRD with a horizontal dipole in tree F and reflector in the North aerial tree E.

c) Communication with CHIRNSIDE 1A used the WS17 with a plain horizontal dipole in the South aerial tree B.

Postscript

The research carried out at Bewley Down began with the dugout and later looked at the involvement of the original owner Douglas Ingrams and the organisation which was behind the development of the site.

There are clear indications that the spy networks in East Devon were set up by the summer of 1940 but were not supported by wireless communication until summer 1942. David Ingrams recalls the construction of the dugout in April 1941 and later its completion which was some twelve months before the arrival of wireless. It was later modified to include the Radio Room.

As a Key Man, with responsibility for his runners and observers, Douglas Ingrams would have been particularly vulnerable without the security and protection of a concealed buried dugout. Unlike battlefield dugouts which provided some protection against bombing and shelling and were camouflaged from the air, the Bewley Down dugout was built to provided concealment against ground searches by Germans. As such, the dugout appears to one of the first of a new class of wartime constructions built for use in areas occupied by an enemy as opposed to those constructed to exclude an enemy and is thus of considerable national interest.

The role of Douglas Ingrams has been studied with family archive material providing an invaluable source of information. There are many gaps in the story of Bewley Down which remain for the time being as every effort has been made to avoid putting forward unsubstantiated theories.

This account is restricted to revealing details of the Bewley Down site and the context within which it operated. It is intended that the sequel to this volume will address many of the wider aspects of the Special Duties Branch modus operandi.

Annex A

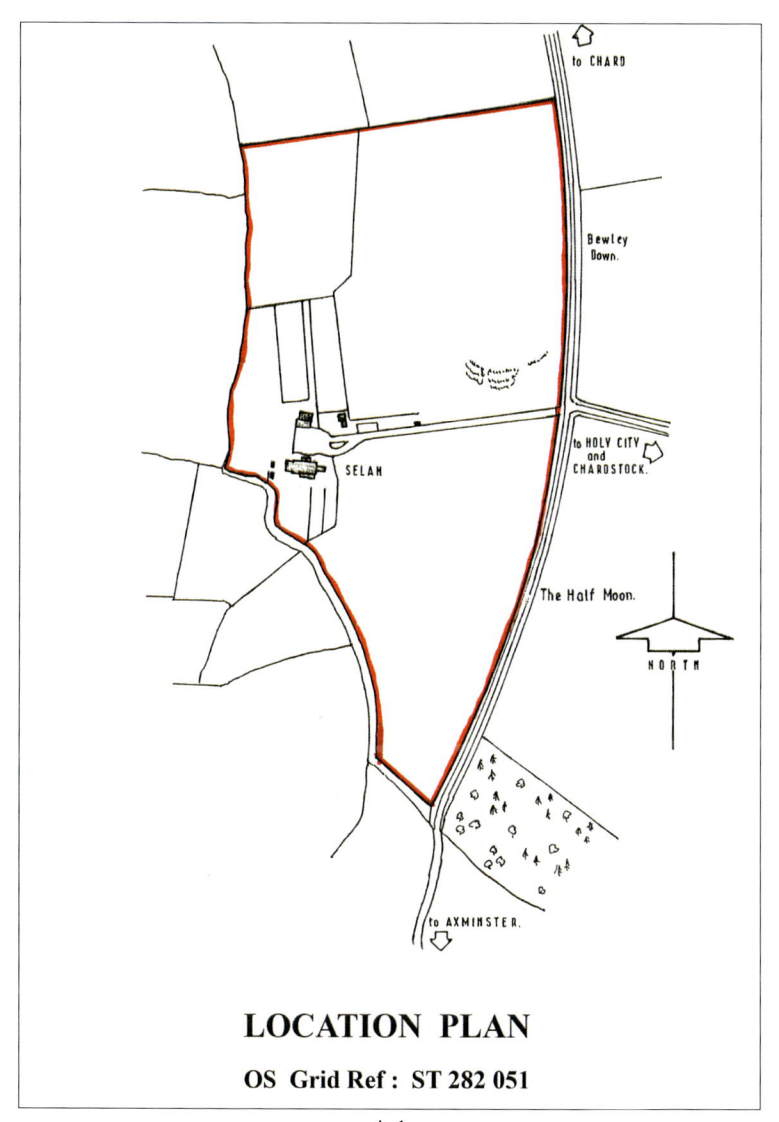

LOCATION PLAN

OS Grid Ref : ST 282 051

A-1

CHIRNSIDE 1

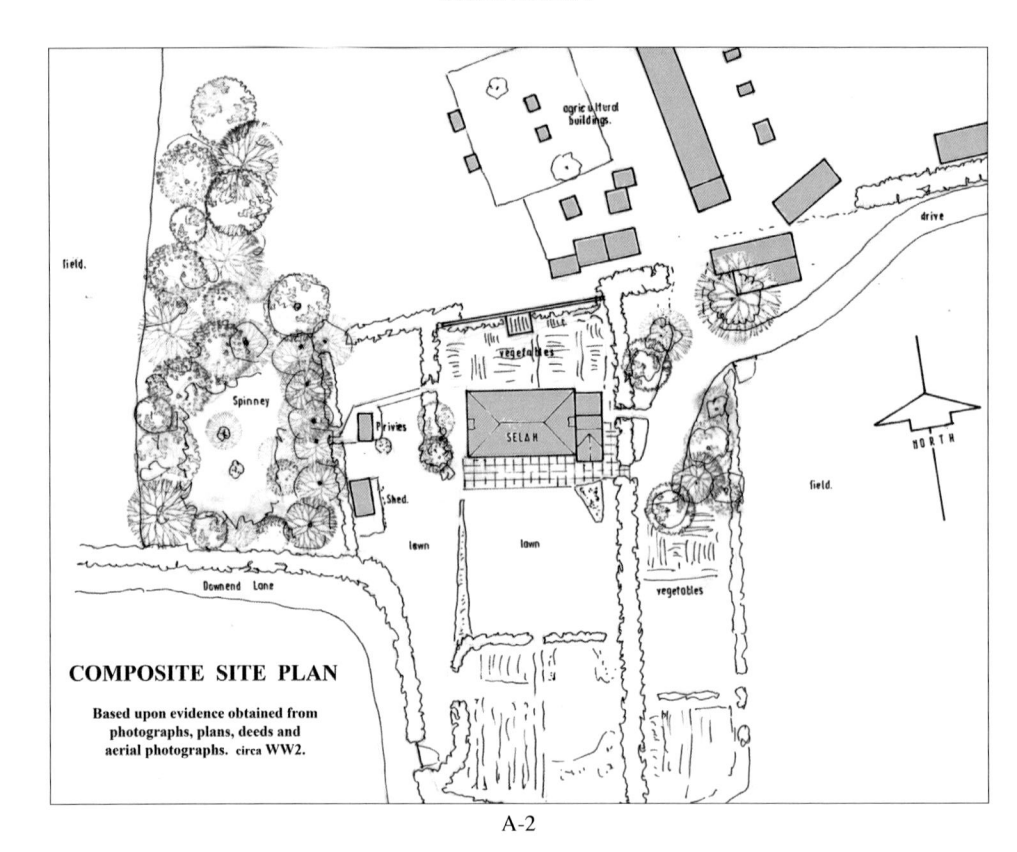

COMPOSITE SITE PLAN

Based upon evidence obtained from
photographs, plans, deeds and
aerial photographs. circa WW2.

Annex A

LAYOUT PLAN
Showing Ventilation and Radio Aerials data.

A-3

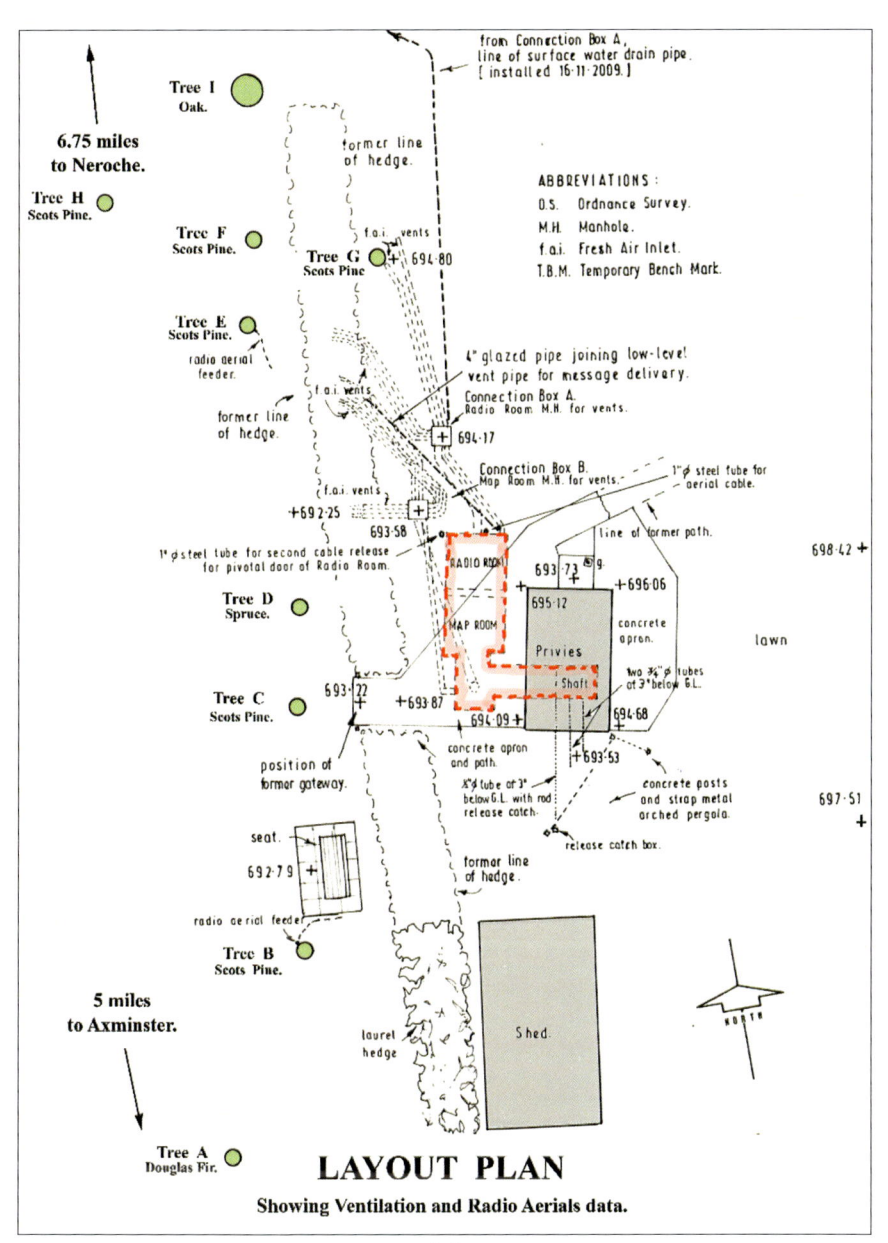

CHIRNSIDE 1

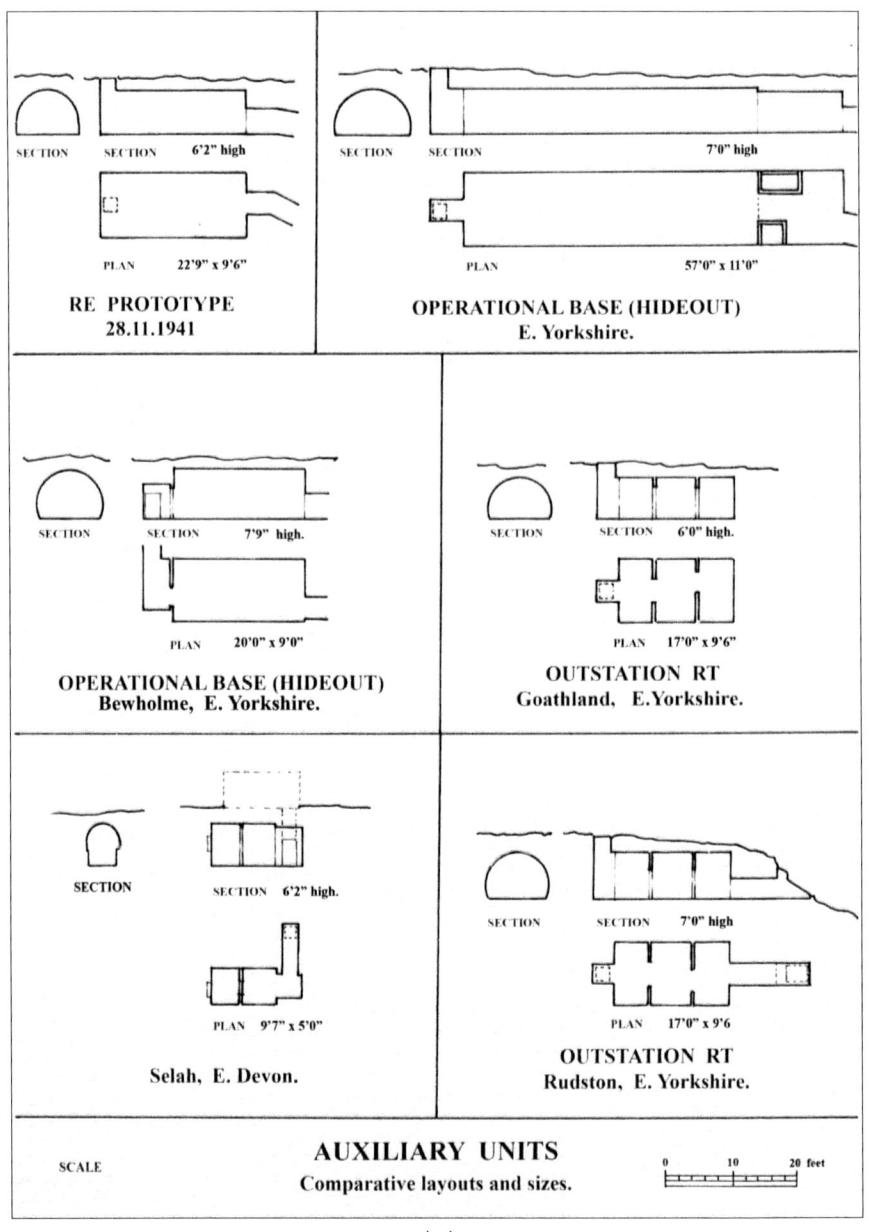

RE PROTOTYPE
28.11.1941

6'2" high
22'9" x 9'6"

OPERATIONAL BASE (HIDEOUT)
E. Yorkshire.

7'0" high
57'0" x 11'0"

OPERATIONAL BASE (HIDEOUT)
Bewholme, E. Yorkshire.

7'9" high.
20'0" x 9'0"

OUTSTATION RT
Goathland, E.Yorkshire.

6'0" high.
17'0" x 9'6"

Selah, E. Devon.

6'2" high.
9'7" x 5'0"

OUTSTATION RT
Rudston, E. Yorkshire.

7'0" high
17'0" x 9'6

AUXILIARY UNITS
Comparative layouts and sizes.

SCALE   0   10   20 feet

A-4

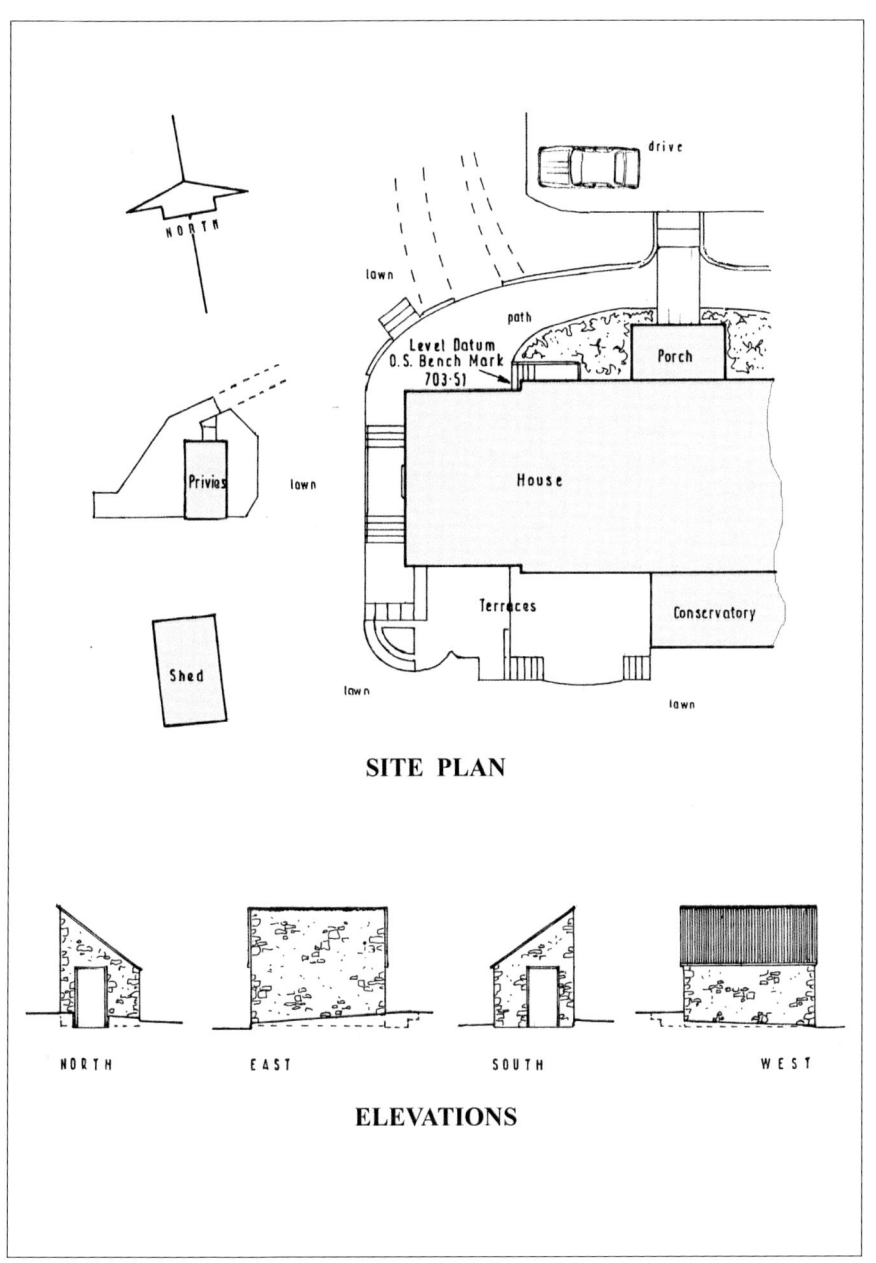

Annex A

SITE PLAN

ELEVATIONS

A-5

CHIRNSIDE 1

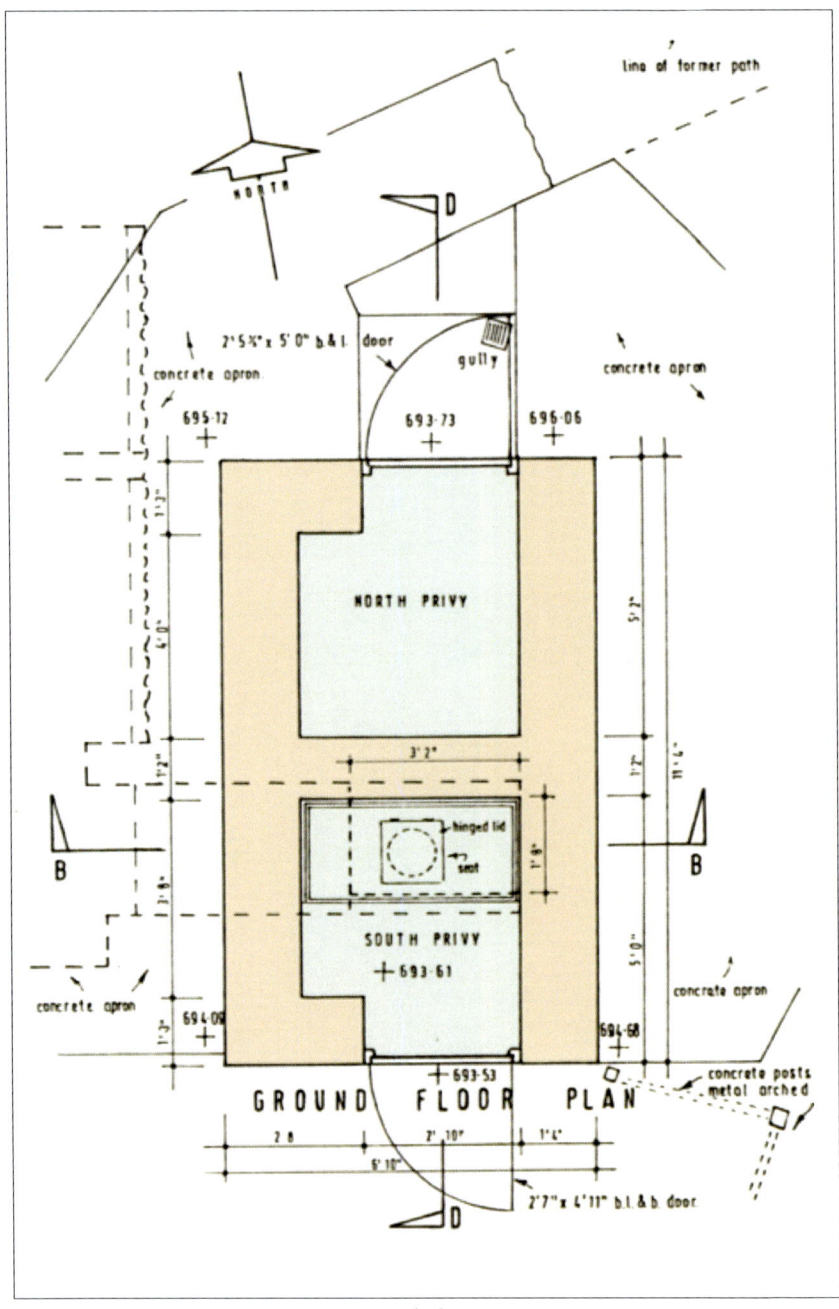

A-6

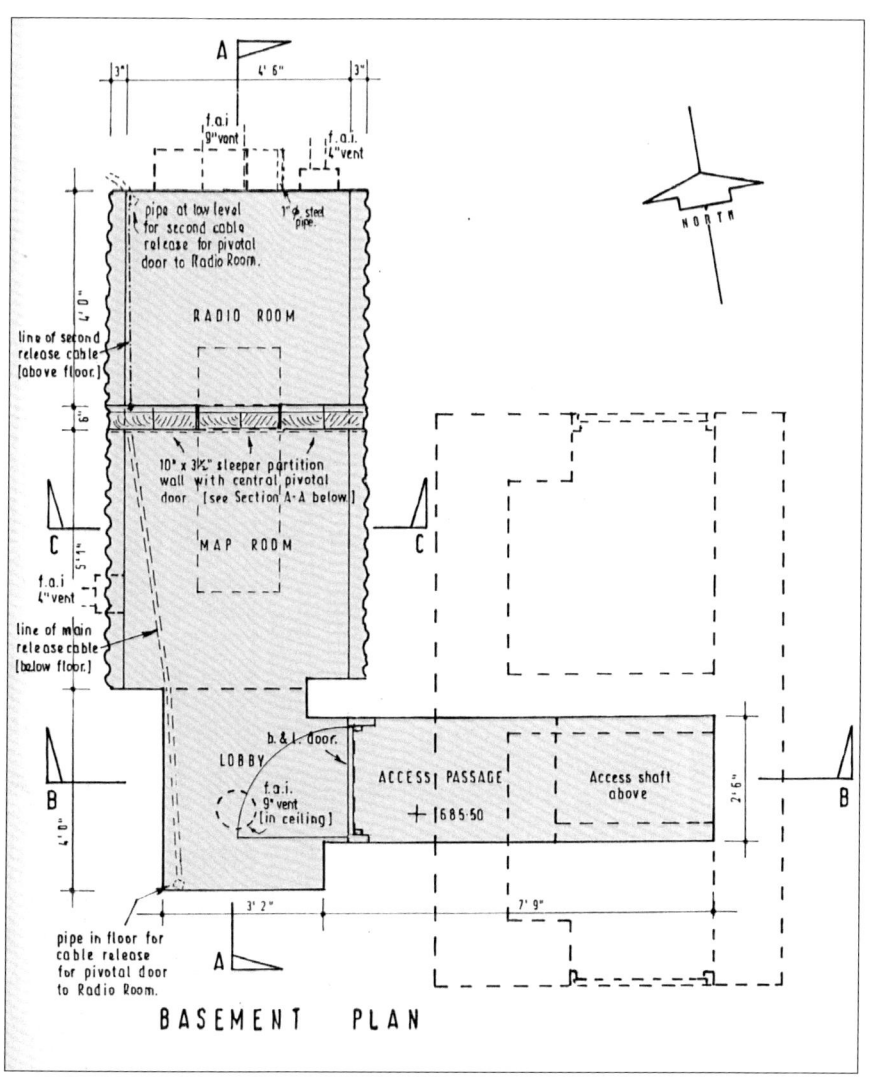

Annex A

A-7

CHIRNSIDE 1

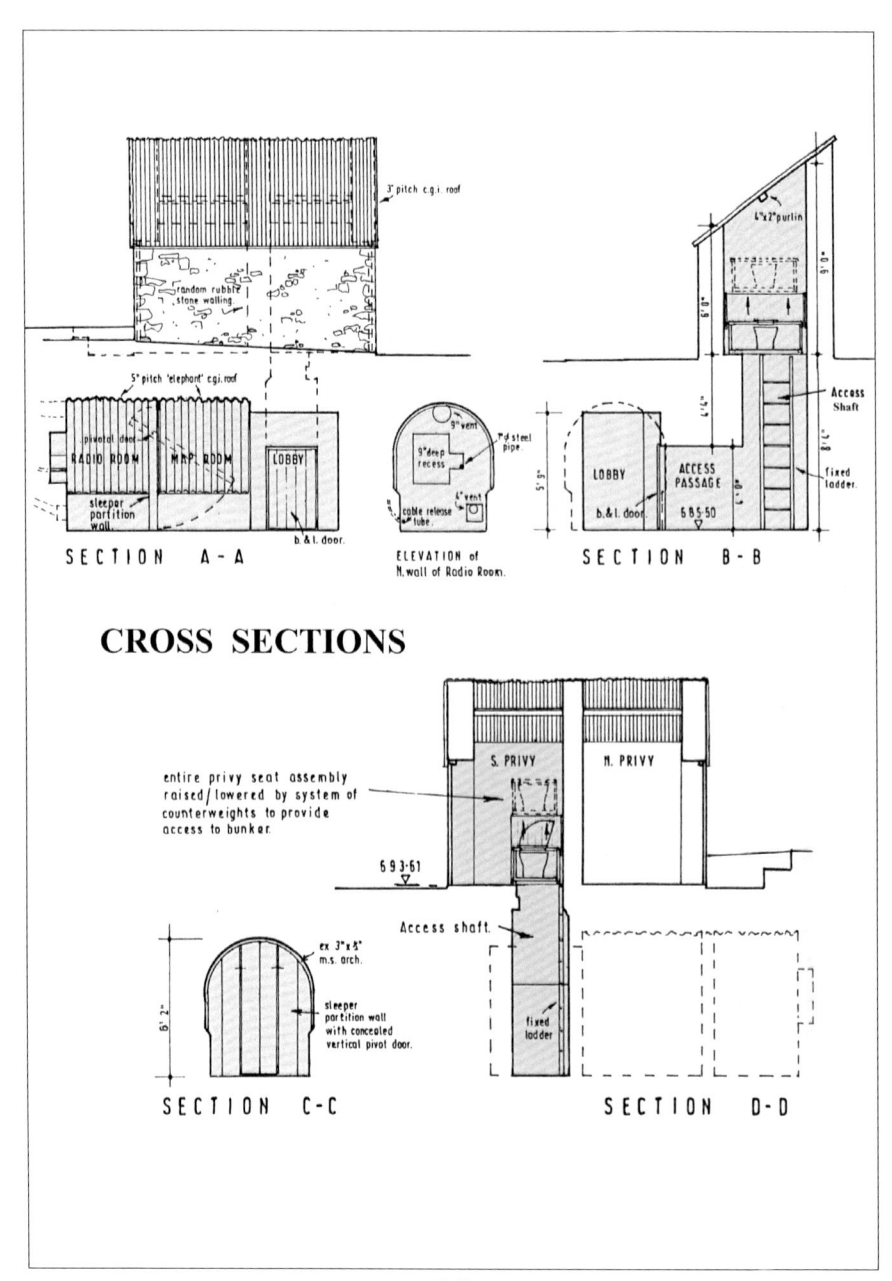

CROSS SECTIONS

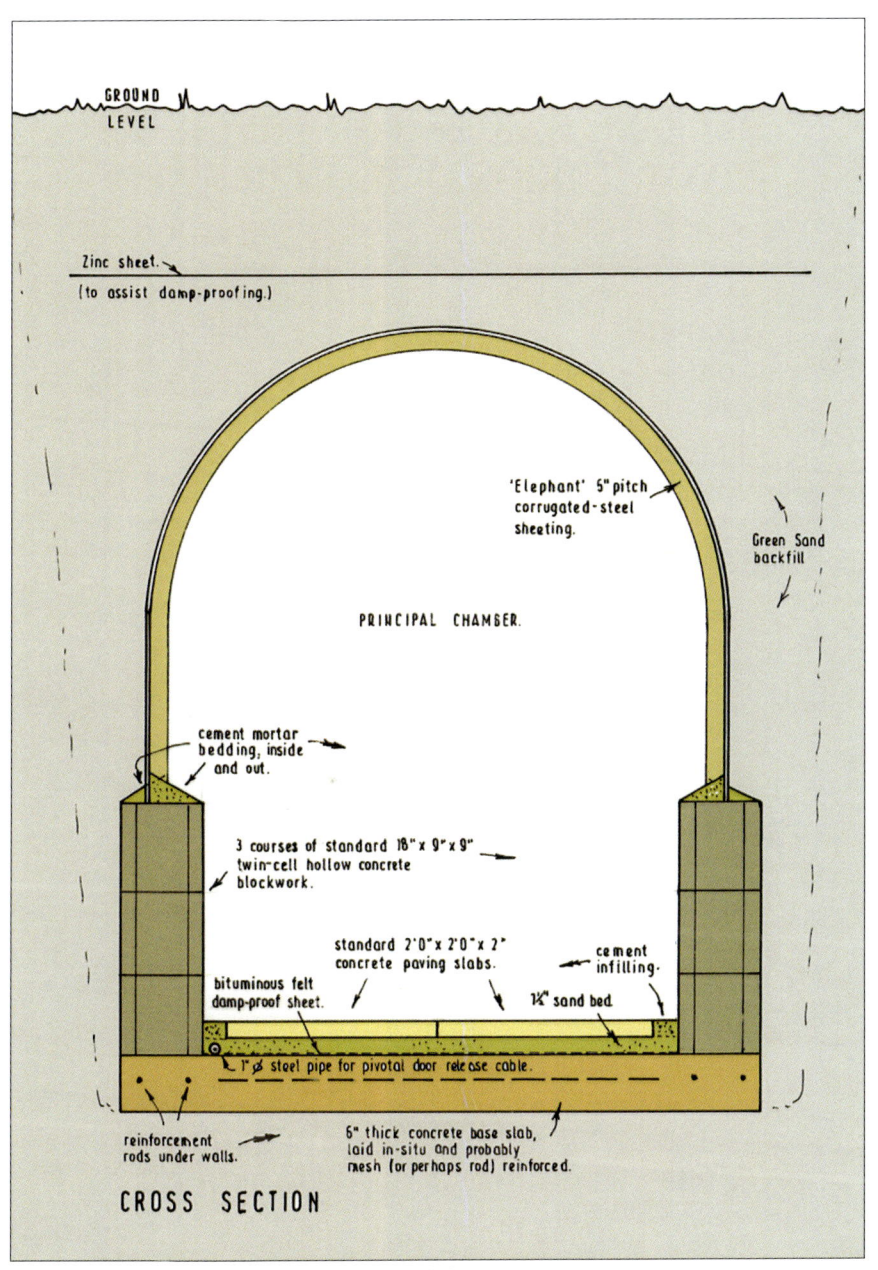

Annex A

A-9

THE SELAH DUGOUT
RELEASE CABLES FOR LATCH ON PIVOTAL DOOR IN SLEEPER WALL.

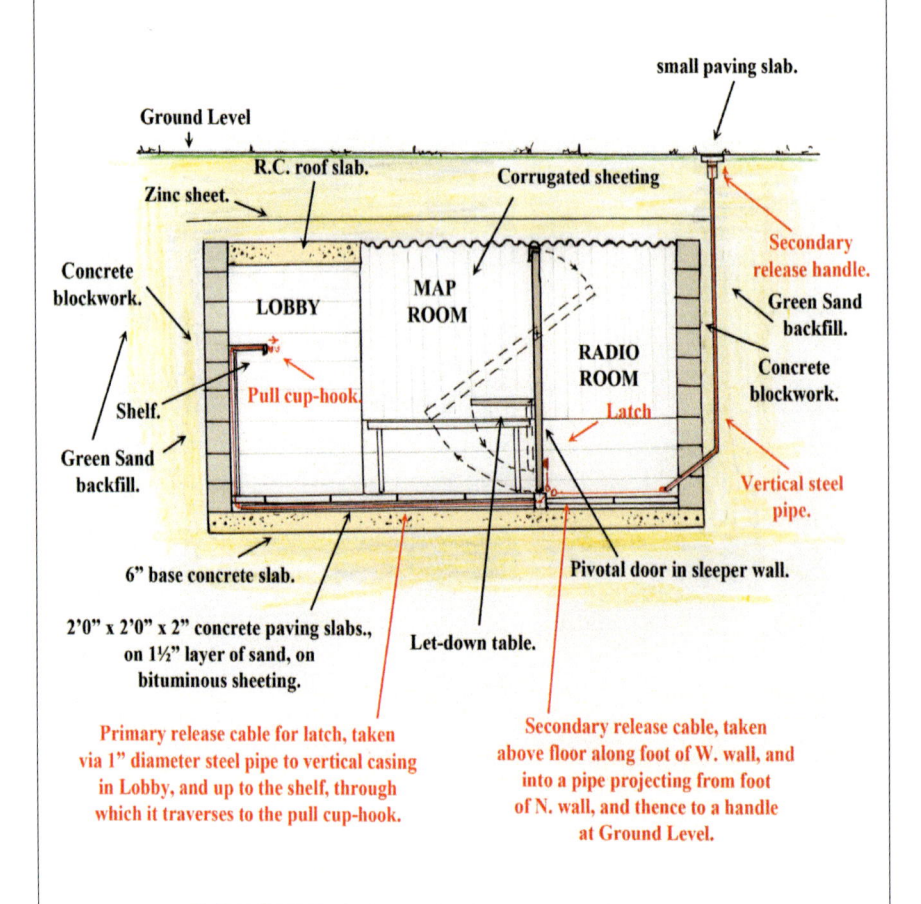

small paving slab.

Ground Level

R.C. roof slab.

Zinc sheet.

Corrugated sheeting

Concrete blockwork.

LOBBY

MAP ROOM

Secondary release handle.

Green Sand backfill.

RADIO ROOM

Concrete blockwork.

Pull cup-hook.

Shelf.

Latch

Green Sand backfill.

Vertical steel pipe.

6" base concrete slab.

Pivotal door in sleeper wall.

2'0" x 2'0" x 2" concrete paving slabs., on 1½" layer of sand, on bituminous sheeting.

Let-down table.

Primary release cable for latch, taken via 1" diameter steel pipe to vertical casing in Lobby, and up to the shelf, through which it traverses to the pull cup-hook.

Secondary release cable, taken above floor along foot of W. wall, and into a pipe projecting from foot of N. wall, and thence to a handle at Ground Level.

LONGITUDINAL SECTION THROUGH LOBBY, MAP ROOM AND RADIO ROOM.

A-10

Annex A

THE SELAH DUGOUT SHOWING THE MESSAGE CARRYING PIPE FROM THE TREE STUMP.

Tree stump with swivel lid.

CONNECTION-BOX A

Ground Level

Zinc sheet.

Corrugated sheeting.

9" extract vent pipe.

Pivotal door in sleeper wall.

MAP ROOM

RADIO ROOM

1" diam, steel pipe.

4" inlet vent pipe.

4" Message-carrying pipe.

Escape hatch (?), blocked off with flattened bit of corrugated sheet.

Message-carrying pipe connects into 4" inlet vent pipe.

2"0" x 2"0" x 2" concrete paving slabs on 1½" layer of sand, on bituminous sheeting, on 6" base concrete slab.

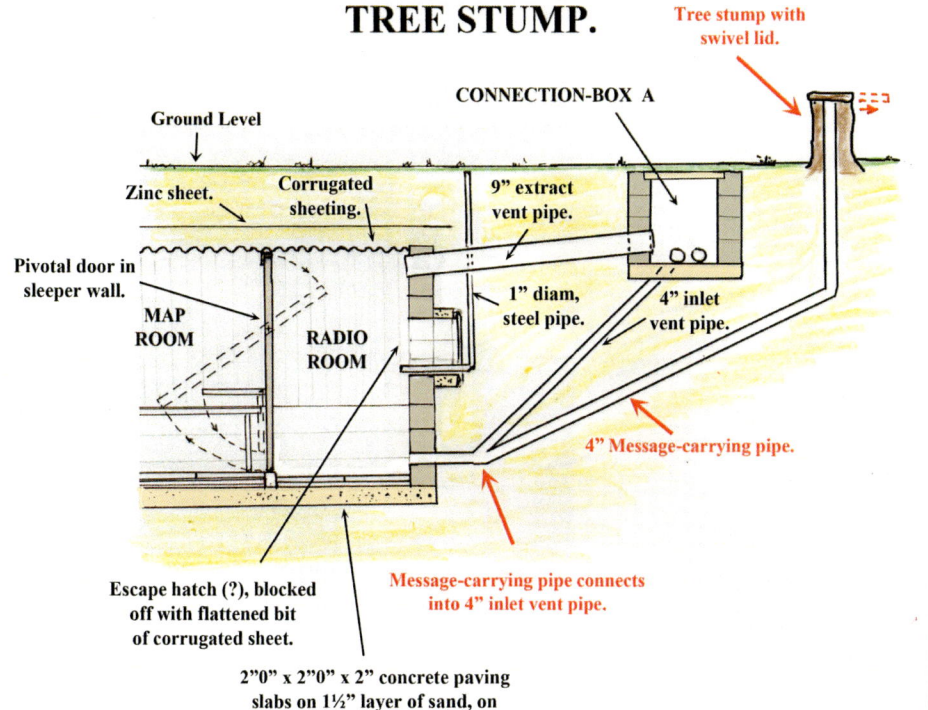

DIAGRAMMATIC LONGITUDINAL SECTION THROUGH RADIO ROOM AND CONNECTION-BOX A.

A-11

CHIRNSIDE 1

Annex B

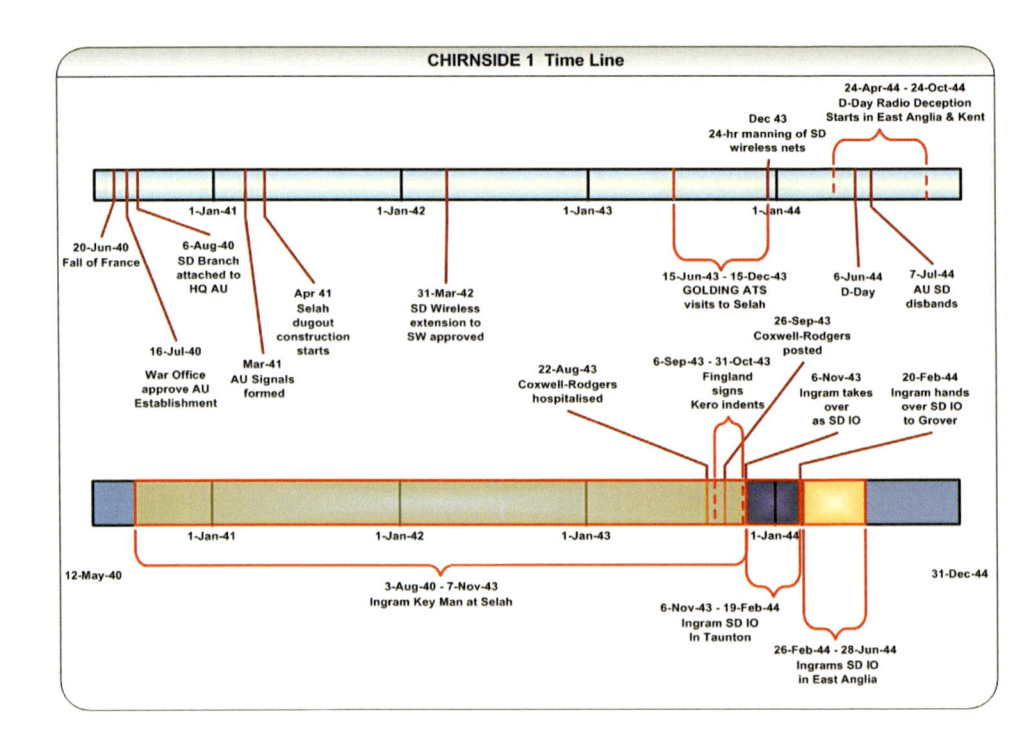

CHIRNSIDE 1 Time Line

- **20-Jun-40** Fall of France
- **16-Jul-40** War Office approve AU Establishment
- **6-Aug-40** SD Branch attached to HQ AU
- **Mar-41** AU Signals formed
- **Apr 41** Selah dugout construction starts
- **31-Mar-42** SD Wireless extension to SW approved
- **22-Aug-43** Coxwell-Rodgers hospitalised
- **15-Jun-43 - 15-Dec-43** GOLDING ATS visits to Selah
- **6-Sep-43 - 31-Oct-43** Fingland signs Kero indents
- **26-Sep-43** Coxwell-Rodgers posted
- **6-Nov-43** Ingram takes over as SD IO
- **Dec 43** 24-hr manning of SD wireless nets
- **6-Jun-44** D-Day
- **7-Jul-44** AU SD disbands
- **24-Apr-44 - 24-Oct-44** D-Day Radio Deception Starts in East Anglia & Kent
- **20-Feb-44** Ingram hands over SD IO to Grover

- **12-May-40** — **31-Dec-44**
- **3-Aug-40 - 7-Nov-43** Ingram Key Man at Selah
- **6-Nov-43 - 19-Feb-44** Ingram SD IO in Taunton
- **26-Feb-44 - 28-Jun-44** Ingrams SD IO in East Anglia

Abbreviations and Glossary

ATS	Auxiliary Territorial Service, the uniformed women's services organisation supporting the Army. Originally a voluntary body which acquired military status in 1941.
AU	Auxiliary Units, the deliberately misleading name given to the GHQ Auxiliary Units which consisted of two parts; the Operational Branch of selected men (primarily from the Home Guard) who were trained to attack German forces from concealed bases after an invasion and the Special Duties Branch that was set up to provided a network of civilian spies to report from areas occupied by the Germans.
Auxiliary	'Other ranks' of the ATS.
	also
	Used as an adjective (e.g. Auxiliary Units, Auxiliary Territorial Service).
Auxilier	Basic term for member of the Auxiliary Units Operational Branch.
Auxiliary Units Signals	Responsible for providing communications to enable civilian observers to pass their information to a military HQ.
BRO	British Resistance Organisation, an entirely modern generic term for AU.
BROM	British Resistance Organisation Museum located at Parham Airfield, Framlingham, Suffolk IP13 9AF
Bunker	Hardened bomb-proof shelter (a German term) often erroneously used to describe an AU underground facility.
'C'	Head of the Secret Service.

CHIRNSIDE 1

Call signs (wireless) — A combination of words or letters and numbers allocated to a wireless station for identity (eg CHIRNSIDE 1). The CONTROL Station of a wireless network is normally call sign 0 (Zero).

Coast watcher(s) — Men attached to the Coastguard Service to watch for shipping and enemy activity including landings and mine laying

or

The AU Special Duties Branch personnel in some coastal areas who maintained a seaward lookout for invaders, (possibly same people).

CONTROL Station — A wireless station (normally an IN-Station) manned by military AU Special Duties Signals personnel who controlled the working of a net or group of wireless stations (OUT-Stations) and received from them intelligence reports.

Denial measures — Military and civilian measures to ensure that an invader could not use ports, railways, waterways, vehicles or telecommunications systems. Where possible facilities were not destroyed thus allowing use after ousting of the invader.

DMI — Director Military Intelligence in the War Office.

Dugout — Underground chamber or passage. Within the Operational Branch they were used for OBs. In the Special Duties Branch they concealed wireless stations.

Dump — A small collection of supplies, stores or ammunition accumulated temporarily for some particular purpose.

GHQ — General Headquarters. The highest level of Army command in a theatre of operations reporting directly to the War Office.

GHQ Home Forces — Command all Army field forces located in the UK. Responsible for the defence of the British Isles and consisted of all corp, divisions and separate units assigned to defend Britain against invasion.

Abbreviations and Glossary

GHQ Auxiliary Units	The title of Auxiliary Units showing that they belonged to GHQ Home Forces. It does not refer to the HQ of GHQ Auxiliary Units.
GPO	General Post Office. A government organisation responsible for postal and telecommunications services.
Group Commanders	Home Guard officers within the Operational Branch each responsible for a number of Operational patrols and reporting to the Operational IOs.
HF	High Frequency (Radio).
HG	Home Guard. See LDV.
Hideout	Original term for concealed underground base for Operational patrols. Considered too indicative of their activities and replaced by Operational Base (OB).
Home Defence Organisation	A closely coordinated sabotage and intelligence network created by Section D of the SIS. Short lived but generally thought to have been the forerunner of AU Special Duties.
HQ	Headquarters.
HQ GHQ Aux Units	Full title of the unit HQ of Auxiliary Units.
HQ AU	Abbreviated title of the unit HQ of Auxiliary Units.
Int	Intelligence.
IN-Station	Wireless station that controlled a network of OUT-Stations and received their intelligence reports. Manned by Royal Signals soldiers or ATS officers.
IO	Intelligence Officer.
Key Man	Originally a position held within the Home Defence Organisation. Within AU Special Duties responsible for each network of observers, runners and associated OUT-Station.
LDV	Local defence volunteers (original name for the Home Guard between May and July 1940.)

MI 5	The British security service dealing with counter-espionage within the UK. Originally a branch of Military Intelligence in the War Office.
MI 6	The British security service dealing with overseas espionage. Originally a branch of Military Intelligence in the War Office.
MI 14	The British security service dealing with Germany. Originally sub-section of MI 3.
OB	Operational base, name given to a dugout of the Operational Patrols of GHQ Home Forces Auxiliary Units.
Observation Units	The cover name for the forerunners of Auxiliary Units in Kent.
Observer	Part time civilian recruited and trained to obtain and pass on intelligence in German occupied areas.
Operational Branch	Selected trained men (primarily from the Home Guard) who after invasion were to attack German logistics behind the front line from a concealed OB.
OUT-Station	Concealed civilian manned wireless station (one man), part of a network communicating with an IN-Station.
Patrol	A team of Auxiliers (5 in number, later 7) which formed the basic unit of the Operational Branch. Role to sabotage German logistic and supply chains. Each patrol had its own OB.
PRO	Public Record Office, official collection of government and court records (from 2003 part of The National Archives (TNA).
Raids	Enemy airborne or seaborne landings of a limited force with the object of destroying vital installations or removing secret equipment and then within hours withdrawing by sea.
RE	Royal Engineers (full title Corps of Royal Engineers) Also known as 'Sappers'.

Regional Commissioners	12 Civil Defence Regions were set up pre war each under a Regional Commissioner through whom Army commanders conveyed their requirements to civilians and civil organisations. Commissioners had wide authority to act if communications with central government were disrupted.
RELAY Station	A manned wireless station that manually retransmits (relays) messages by wireless between wireless stations that are unable to communicate directly.
	or
	An unmanned wireless station that automatically retransmits wireless messages (rebroadcasts) to other wireless stations on the same or different frequency.
Reserved occupation	A government list of occupations which allowed employers to apply for men (and later women) to be deferred from call-up into the Armed Forces since they worked in industries or occupations that were important to the war effort or life of the community.
RF	Radio frequency.
RT	Radio telephone or radio telephony voice communications.
Runner	Civilian recruited and trained to collect reports left by observers in dead letter drops and deliver them to another dead letter drop.
Scout Sections	Sub-units of about 12 regular infantry soldiers tasked with assisting and training Auxiliary Units Operational patrols.
	Normally 2 sections per county.
Special Duties Branch	Military personnel of Special Duties Organisation.
Special Duties Organisation	A collective term for the military personnel of the Special Duties Branch and the civilians working under key men as observers or runners.

CHIRNSIDE 1

SDS	Modern abbreviation of Special Duties Section, a term and abbreviation not used in contemporary documentation.
Section D	The first dirty tricks department of the Secret Intelligence Service with a remit to operate clandestinely against the enemy in a non-attributable way.
SIS	Secret Intelligence Service. Government agency dealing with foreign intelligence. Commonly known as MI 6.
SUB-OUT-Station	A civilian manned wireless station that passes information by a separate wireless link to a local OUT-Station which it then relayed to the IN-Station.
SOE	Special Operations Executive. Approved by War Cabinet on 22 July 1940 'to coordinate all action, by way of subversion and sabotage, against the enemy overseas'.
TA	Territorial Army. Voluntary reserve force of the British Army.
TNA	The National Archives, formerly the Public Record Office.
TRD	The nomenclature for the VHF wireless transmitter/receiver used between IN-Stations and OUT-Stations.
VHF	Very high frequency (radio transmission).
War Establishments Committee	War Office committee that decided the allocation of manpower, ATS women, weapons and vehicles to which units were entitled in wartime.
WO	War Office, the executive department of State responsible for the Army. Also the abbreviation in the National Archives catalogue for records created or inherited primarily by the War Office.
WS17	Wireless Set No.17. A small VHF voice transmitter/receiver used by searchlight units and adopted for use by AU for communication links between OUT-Stations and SUB-OUT-Stations.

ZERO Station An AU Signals term for a concealed underground IN-Station in a dugout, equipped to operate completely closed down for 21 days if German troops occupied the area. The call sign of a CONTROL Station running a wireless net is normally ZERO for both above and underground installations.

Note: *A variety of terms and abbreviations relating to Auxiliary Units are currently in use, some of which conflict. In some cases authors have adopted differing terminology. The terms in the above 'Abbreviations and Glossary' have been extracted from WWII contemporary records, principally WO manuals and HQAU papers on PRO files and are believed to reflect the terminology originally in use.*

Selected Bibliography and Data Source

Fleming, P. *Invasion 1940,* Rupert Hart-Davis, 1957

Fleming, P. *Invasion 1940*, Akadine Press, 2000

Gabbitas, A. *AU wireless,* Article

Hunt, D. *various references,* 2008

Ingrams, D. *German Invasion – British Resistance*, Lecture notes, 1996

Ingrams, D. *Letter to Dr.W. Ward,* Jan 19th. 1997

Lampe, D. *The Last Ditch*, Cassell, 1968

Mackenzie, S. P. *The Home Guard,* Oxford University Press, 1995

Oxenden, N. Auxiliary Units History and Achievement 1940-1944, BROM, 1998

The National Archives, *Numerous references*

Ward, A. *Resisting the Nazi Invader,* Constable, 1997

Warren, D. *Now you see it-Then you didn't,* SIAS survey 14, 2004

Warwicker, J. *Churchill's Underground Army*, Frontline, 2008

Warwicker, J. *South-Western Sortie,* BROM, 1999

Warwicker, J. *With Britain in Mortal Danger*, Cerberus, 2000

Index

A

Aerials, 80
  feeder cables, 82
  north trees, 84, 89
  south tree, 90, 91
Alexander, Mary, 12
AU Operational Branch, 2
  chain of command, 3
  Group Commanders, 3
  Intelligence Officer, 2
  Patrol Leaders, 3
  Patrols, 3, 10
  role after invasion, 2
  Scout Sections, 3
AU Signals, 11
ATS Officers, 12
  establishment, 12
AU Special Duties Branch, 2, 4, 5
  chain of command, 6
  deployment and role, 7
  Dugouts, 15, 35
  not retained, 22
  Observer, 4, 6
  personnel, 5, 13
  Runner, 4, 6, 8
  War Establishment, 5
AU Special Duties Organisation, 5, 11
  disbandment, 14
Auxiliary Territorial Service (ATS), 1
Auxiliary Units(AU)
  7 Whitehall Place, 2
  close down, 15

B

Bachelor's Hall, 11
Badgerow, Priscilla, 12
Bewley Down, 13, 16, 26, 27, 32, 74, 80, 83, 88
Briscoe's Farm, 88
British Expeditionary Force (BEF), 1
British Resistance Organisation (BRO), 8, 27
British Secret Services, 1

C

CHIRNSIDE 1: 12, 34, 88
  24hr manning, 80
Coleshill House, 2, 5
Collings, Maj. J, 22, 80
Commando Units, 1
Coxwell-Rogers, Capt. C, 7, 21

D

D-Day
  role of Special Duties Organisation, 10
Dead letter drops, 8
Deane, Dickie, 16
Defence Medal, 14, 27
Defence of Britain Project, 27
Delmer, Sefton, 21
Douglas, Col. FWR, 14

E

Eames, Medora, 27

F

Franklyn, General HE, 10, 22

G

General Headquarters (GHQ) Home Forces, 1, 5
GHQ Auxiliary Units, 1
Grover, Capt. EC, 22, 80
Gubbins, Col. C McV, 2, 3, 5, 21

H

Hannington Hall, 5
Hills, Capt. J, 11
Holland, Lt.Col. JFC, 21
Home Guard, 2, 9, 14
Honours Committee, 14

I

Ingrams
   David, 9, 17, 26, 31, 88
   Doreen, 20
   Douglas, 7, 8, 12, 17, 20, 21, 26, 80
   Eileen Patricia, 20
   Harold, 20
   Leonard, 20
   Rev. WS, 20
   visitors' book, 12, 80
IN-Station, 8, 11
   Castle Neroche, 12, 74, 88
   Volis Farm, 80
Irregular Warfare, 1

K

Key Men, 6, 7, 10, 11

M

Military Intelligence, 1
   MI6, 2
   Section D, 21
Moore, Myrtle, 27
Moulton-Barrett, Florence, 17

O

Observation Units, 2
Official Secrets Act, 7
OUT-Station, 8, 11. *See also* CHIRNSIDE 1
   Sigglesthorne, 84, 96
Oxenden, Maj. NV, 2, 9, 10

P

Petherick, Maj. M, 5
Political Warfare Executive (PWE), 21
Privy, xiv, xv, xvi, 34, 40, 42, 63 *et seq*, 78, 79
Pyrland Hall, 12

R

Raiders, 10
Royal Signals technicians, 13

S

Saudi Royalty
   King Faisal, 24
Secret Intelligence Service (SIS), 2, 5
SELAH, 9, 12, 16, 39
SELAH Dugout
   access passage, 34
   access shaft, 34
   communication, 60
   concealment, 40
   costing considerations, 72
   field telephone, 78
   flooding, 39
   general description, 31
   later construction, 51
   lighting & heating, 39, 77, 78, 79
   lobby, 34
   map room, 51
   measured survey, xii, 39, 40, 65, 71
   radio room, 51
   restoration, 40
   seat box, 40, 41
   security anomalies, 65
   sleeper wall, 51, 52
   structural anomalies, 63
   ventilation, 35
Shortt
   Doreen, 20
   Eileen, 20
   Sir Edward, 20
Somerset Industrial Archaeological Society, 27
Special Communications Unit, 15
Special Operations Executive (SOE), 1
SUB-OUT-Station, 12, 74, 96

W

Ward, Capt. K, 11, 75, 87
Warren, D, 27
Warwicker, J, 27
Wireless
   availability, 4
   basic network, 13
   basic system, 11
   networks, 8, 11
   sets destroyed, 15
   TRD transceiver, 74, 90, 97
Wireless Set 17 (WS17), 13, 74,